Britney Fairweather's TALL TALES

Jaclyn Aurore

MORNING RAIN PUBLISHING

Britney Fairweather's Tall Tales

By

Jaclyn Aurore

Copyright 2014 by Jaclyn Aurore
Cover design copyright 2014 by Morning Rain Publishing

ISBN: 978-1-928133-13-1

Acknowledgements

I'd like to thank my hubby for the wonderful support and encouragement - when the rejections came pouring in, you inspired me and motivated me to continue. Without you, Britney would just be collecting dust in my closet - a memory waiting to be stolen.

Dedication

To my young sisters - I hope your adventures are just as magical as Britney's.

Table of Contents

Britney Fairweather and the Blue Fairy

The buzzer on my alarm rings through the room. After smacking it around a few times, I'm finally able to find the button to turn it off. Rolling to my side and putting my back to the clock, I try with all my might to return to the dream I was having prior to the rude awakening.

Focussing on my breathing, I let my mind go blank. It's not long before I see the blue orb shadow that tells me I'm right where I want to be – flying in the air, weaving between trees. My magic wand, made by sprinkling fairy dust on an old oak tree branch, is firmly within my grasp. This is freedom, though I don't feel free. I feel hurt, like I'm suffering from a bullet wound to the chest, but after close inspection, I realize there is none. Nothing external anyway, but it's definitely heartache I feel as I fly through The Enchanted Forest. Heartache and loneliness. Lost without a sense of purpose.

Though I know that I'm searching for something, I have no idea what it is I hope to find. Just when the fog in my mind begins to clear, the bloody alarm clock goes off again, and I realize that I hit 'snooze' instead of 'off'.

"ARGHHH!" I yell, kicking my feet under my duvet and accidentally startling my dog, Mustard. "Why is the alarm even set, boy? It's Saturday! The only day I'm allowed to actually sleep in, and I've forgotten to unset the alarm. What was I thinking?"

Mustard makes his way to my bedroom door as I hit the correct button on the clock, three times just to be sure it won't disrupt me again. It's too late now though, I can't go back to sleep. My dog is pawing at the door, and I know he needs to be let out. "Bathroom breaks for both of us, Musty… but me first, okay?"

I open my door and make my way to the bathroom as my golden labradoodle bolts for the kitchen. He's pretty good about waiting there for me to let him out the backdoor, but my mom is usually close by, the kitchen being her haven. I'm confident she'll let him out before I'm even done my morning routine of pee, flush, hands, teeth, hair… sometimes shower, but not today.

Today I have a story to tell. That dream was just too vivid; I need to write it down. I need to remember every detail I can because it wasn't me I dreamt about; it was the Blue Fairy.

It wasn't with ease that I left my home in Belgrove. Life just didn't suit me there. The further I flew from the only forest I knew, the harder it was on my heart. Strings were very clearly pulling me back, but stubborn as I am, I needed to fly onward. The fairies are a loyal bunch, myself included, except when the only boy I ever loved proposed to my sister, I had to flee.

She is not to blame; neither is he. This is just how it is. Fairies must be paired in the order of their birth. My sister, Bloom, was next in line to be courted. I wasn't supposed to even show interest in anyone until it was my turn, but I'd known Onyx for most of my life. We were the best of friends. He had not even met my sister until two moons before they were joined.

Onyx was my best kept secret. We met in the hollow of a great oak tree that was hidden from Belgrove on an almost daily basis. It all started when I met him in that same hollow, completely by accident. He was flying carelessly away from his home in Candun and had come dangerously close to the trail the humans took regularly. Sure, humans can't see us, but their dogs can. On this fateful day, Onyx was spotted by an unleashed four-legged fur ball that proceeded to chase him into hiding.

Unsure of his safety, he stayed hidden in the hollow he had randomly found. This is the story he told me when I flew in there out of curiosity. Belgrove and Candun are two of the five fairy territories that share this particular Enchanted Forest; it's not uncommon for our tribes to run into each other – but in an unmarked tree? This seemed like fate.

We became fast friends. I didn't even realize my feelings were growing for him. His older brother was unmatched as well, so courting wasn't something either of us could do. As a male though, he probably hadn't even considered it. So as my feelings evolved, they went unnoticed and unreturned. As my heart grew for him, I knew we should stop meeting in the hollow, but I couldn't bring myself to be without him. I tried. I tried to visualize what it'd be like to never see him again, to never fly with him, to never cast harmless spells of confusion on the human trails, to never pick berries from the bushes in the Fair Fox territory... I tried.

The problem was that Onyx felt as much a part of me as the rest of the forest. Each time I told myself I wouldn't fly to him,

I did it anyway. Each time I told myself that it didn't matter if he felt the same way, I knew I was lying. Each time I tried to convince myself that one day he'd fall in love with me… those were the times I'd fly. Those were the times I'd answer his whistle. Knowing we were second in line to be matched, and that it wasn't unreasonable for us to be together, made all the lying and sneaking away from my family in Belgrove to be with him… well it made it all worth it.

I loved Onyx. I loved him more than myself. He was the one… and then he wasn't.

The forbidden love that we had – well, that I had – was bearable because I had convinced myself that the only reason we weren't together was because it wasn't yet time. The time was coming nearer though; Onyx's older brother had announced that he'd be matched in one moon. Once Bloom was matched, or at least betrothed, then Onyx could share his feelings for me. I had hope, as I was certain that was the only reason he hadn't yet presented the idea of us being romantic.

My heart grew two sizes that day. My time was coming, even if Onyx didn't know it yet. There was a skip to my flight… that must have been what caused a spark of curiosity for Bloom. She never in her whole fairy life gave a flying flit about me, but that day she stealthily flew behind me, tracking my moves.

And I paid so little attention. I had no idea she was behind me; my focus was only on what was in front… Onyx and our hollow.

I was very close to my favourite oak tree when I heard, "Anemone! Where on earth are you going?"

The sound of my sister's voice had startled me mid-flight. Attempting to simultaneously change directions before she found my tree, and turn to see where her placement was in the air, caused me to become disoriented. For the first time in my life, I crashed and ended up flying head first into the oak I was trying to avoid. Not able to collect my bearings in time, I plummeted to the earth. The only thing that saved me from death was the pile of leaves I'd landed in.

Every day since then, I wished there were no leaves in The Enchanted Forest. Death would have been better than what came next.

Bloom, the fairy that she was, noticed the hollow before noticing her own sister's predicament. She flew into it just as Onyx popped his head out. "Anna? Is that you?" he asked.

I tried to call out to him from the ground, but my voice was lodged in my throat. All that screaming had taken out a lung. "I'm down here," I whispered.

Naturally, Onyx didn't hear my response. Bloom had hovered directly in front of him, and that was all he could see.

"Tsk, tsk. You aren't Anna Softsong."

"I most certainly am not. Anemone is my immature, careless, naïve little sister. I am Bloom Softsong. Who might you be?"

"Onyx Riverbend. Pleasure to meet you, Bloom. Welcome to my humble hollowed hide-away."

And just like that, I was forgotten. Bloom flew into the hollow of the oak tree with Onyx, leaving me below to tend to my damaged wing. With the help of a fire ant, I was able to fly within the hour. In that time, the two fairies in the hollow never left. I could hear them giggling and laughing and flirting... I could hear them complimenting each other from my spot on the ground. Not once did either of them ask where I was. Considering that Bloom had seen me fall, it surprised me a little that she didn't think to search for me. But it was Onyx's lack of concern that broke my heart.

I flew back to the Belgrove territory without saying goodbye to the two hidden in the tree. Avoiding the eyes of any other fairy I passed, and the voices of my tribe as I crossed the border into my home, I flew to the top of the tree my family called home, and beyond the branch that I've come to use as my bed. I didn't stop flight until I reached the topmost leaf.

Remaining there for days, avoiding, too, the pangs of hunger, I refused to come down from my unsafe perch. On the sixth day, my father had sent out a search, and the bluebird gave away my position. She hadn't done it out of spite, I know this because she told me. She was concerned for my wellbeing. If I went any longer without food, I would have fallen from the top with no chance of surviving the drop, leaves to catch me or not...

If my heart wasn't broken enough, I learned the reason why my father sent a search party. It wasn't because he was concerned for me and my safety as the bluebird had been; it was to announce that he had been asked permission by a Candun fairy for the blessing of courtship. My dad granted Onyx his request and the date was set. Within two moons, my lovely sister, Bloom, would be matched to the only boy I ever loved.

I had known the day would come, but it still hurt. Though my wings were fixed, my heart had shattered to an unrepairable state on the day of the fall. Onyx would never be with me. He never loved me. He never saw me as anything other than the blue fairy who had accidentally flown into his hidey-hole.

I had falsely convinced myself that I had a chance with him... that he was only waiting until I was technically available… that one day he'd ask my father his permission to court me. My worst nightmare had not prepared me for even the slightest inclination that he'd court my sister instead.

Being the good, loyal fairy that I am, I attended the ceremony that matched my older sister to the love of my life. The minute I thought my life couldn't get any worse, that my heart couldn't possibly break anymore, I witnessed the matching that I failed to see coming.

They spent their after-match retreat in the hidden hallow of the oak. It became their oak, and they had told their respective tribes that they would be living in the oak on the edge of the human trail, a place unclaimed by any tribe in the woods. Neither had thought to ask me how I felt about this. In a way, I had claimed it as mine, but as I'm not a tribe on my own I couldn't lay claim to a tree that I wanted. As a matched pair, they were entitled to lay claim to any available tree. Since the secret hide-away had been in a stretch of land between territories, Onyx and Bloom became their very own tribe.

Knowing I lost absolutely everything I held dear, I decided to flee. I denounced my name as Anemone Softsong, fairy of the Belgrove tribe, and flew directly south until I passed the border of the Enchanted Realm and entered the paved land of the humans. This hadn't been done by any of the tribes before, but I had nothing left to lose. I didn't care about the danger the paved world presented, the mechanics of the humans, or the humans themselves. Magic might disguise my shape leaving me invisible to all who disbelieved, but it didn't leave me shielded from touch. I was just as capable of flying into things in the paved world as I was in the woods. The chances of this happening were greater outside the forest because we didn't know the realms. It's the number one reason why we never left. That, and we're creatures of habit and habitat. We have no natural desires to drift to the unknown.

I had no desire to stay.

My body continued to break, the further I got from my realm, but it also felt alive… like a weight had been lifted from me. I had no cause, no purpose to my life, anymore. I hadn't a care in the world, and I never felt more invigorated.

I'd never be whole again… I'd never fall in love again… I'd never let myself get attached again… and I'd never have a name again. From then on, I would only be known as the colour of my glow, the colour of the flower that I was named after, and coincidentally the mood I would indefinitely be in – from this point on, I would only be known as the Blue Fairy.

After putting my pen down, I crawl back into my bed and bury myself underneath the covers. It isn't long before Mustard takes his rightful place at the foot of my bed, making it difficult for me to roll over without kicking him, but simultaneously making sure that my feet are warm.

"You're the best dog in the world, Mustard. I may never fall in love, or worse, I may fall in love and have my heart shattered into a million tiny pieces, but as long as I have you, I have purpose. I have reason to be happy. Thanks, boy."

Mustard is really good at reading emotions. He can sense that I'm sad, feeling the sting of loneliness sent to me by the Blue Fairy. Of course, he doesn't know why I feel this way; I certainly have no reason to be upset. He cuddles me regardless, shifting from my feet, slithering up beside me like a snake, placing one heavy paw on my chest, and licking a long line from my chin to my forehead.

His tongue has a magical way of making me feel both

better and gross, all in one go, but at least he successfully removed the pain from my heart.

"Ew! Mustard!" I can't even scold him properly as I begin to laugh uncontrollably.

This tells my dog two things: one, I like being licked, and two; it's time to wake up. Not so snake-like this time, he pounces on top of me and begins slobbering all over my face. Every time I laugh, the weight of the sixty-pound beast crushes me, making it difficult to inhale my next breath. Through fits of giggles, I command, "Off!"

Mustard doesn't need to be told twice. He leaps from the bed and sits in front of me, panting while his tail wags back and forth along the floor.

"You want to go on an adventure, Musty?" I ask using the baby voice I reserve only for him.

In his excitement, he jumps up onto the bed, back to the floor, circles around himself two times, and then sits again, but not for long.

"Alright, alright, I'm coming."

A quick look out my bedroom window tells me that it's sunny with not a cloud in the sky. The fine hairs on my arm that are slightly on edge tell me there's a chance of rain.

"You know what this means?" I ask my dog, who is now sitting not so patiently by my bedroom door. Even though it's open and he can run freely around the house, he still chooses to wait for me.

Scratching under his chin as I reach to the hook on the wall above his head, I finish, "It means we might get to jump in mud puddles!"

I keep my raincoat in my room because it's my favourite. The bright pink polka dots sort of match the yellow polka dots on my rain boots and umbrella, but my favourite part about it is the oversized hood with the piglet ears. It falls in front of my face, keeping me dry but making it difficult to see. At the moment, I have no need for the umbrella that I got with it, which is also a little too big, but I can use my umbrella for other things – like a magical compass that points me in the direction of otherworldly things – so I bring it along.

Sure the rain gear might look like something a little kid would own, especially with the animal ears on the hood, but it came in my size, and I absolutely love it. So I've got no shame in wearing it today, on a day that appears sunny but will soon rain.

"Who will see me in The Enchanted Forest anyway?"

Mustard cocks his head to the side and lets his tongue hang from his mouth.

His comical expression makes me laugh. "Come on, boy, let's pack some snacks and head back to the woods."

Our adventures usually start as a walk. We never really know what we're looking for until we find it. Today is different. Today I want to find the fairies and see if they know anything of the Blue Fairy from my dreams. It may be just that: a dream.

"But it felt so real, Mustard." One of the beauties of having a dog is that you can pass off your ramblings as semi-normal. It's okay to talk to my pet; it's not okay to talk to myself. This is a rule I learned the hard way growing up… too many people make fun of my weirdness.

My pet, however, understands me better than any human

I've met before. Even though I've only spoken half my sentence out loud, Mustard acknowledges with a tilt of his head and a small bark in response. He's more than a pet; he's a companion. Mustard is my best friend, loyal and loving, and he has the best nose on the planet.

"What's that you smell, boy?" I ask as I watch him sniff the ground.

Of course, he doesn't answer me, but he does keep his nose to the ground as he leaves the trail and sniffs his way into the heart of the forest. I'm not worried about getting lost, though it is easy to do. Mustard can always find his way back home, no matter how deep we travel.

"Best nose on the planet, right, boy?"

He lifts his head from the ground, pants, barks, and resumes his search. The sun is still shining, so I don't quite need my umbrella yet, but if Mustard is on to something magical, my umbrella will act as a compass.

Since the yellow polka dot umbrella has a hook for a handle and is long and thin when collapsed, I'm able to carry it by shoving it through the belt buckle on my jeans. When it's not raining, the umbrella dangles by my leg like a sword, ready to be drawn at the first drop. If I'm still outside when it stops raining, I'll give it a good shake and hook the handle through the belt loop once more, usually resulting in a wet leg. Ginger Bean, the nickname I've affectionately given my mother, hasn't quite figured out how I manage to come home with only half my pants wet.

"Not today though, it's going to be a nasty storm; I can feel it." I unhook the umbrella from my pants and point the tip in the direction my dog is sniffing. "As soon as it starts, Mustard, we'll have to head on back. We don't want to be caught out here in a torrential downpour. We'll be soaked from head to toe."

Normally the dog responds to me somehow, with a soft bark or a cocked head, but this time he ignores me completely as he makes a ninety-degree turn, following his nose. My umbrella tugs gently in the same direction, so I know Mustard is on to something magical.

Following both the dog and the magical compass blindly, I look to the sky to see if there's any sign of rain. Through the tangled web of tree branches, I see nothing but blue – not a cloud in sight. "Soon, boy. When it comes, it'll come fast."

After another turn right, though this time not as sharp, Mustard begins sniffing the base of a tall oak tree. I can't quite tell if he's found something, or if he's just found the perfect spot to pee. Just as I convince myself it's the latter, my umbrella points upward to the nearest branch and springs open. I grab the umbrella's hook handle with both hands, but the force is too strong. It slips from my grip and shoots up into the tree way out of reach. Not only that, but I'd been using my whole body to try to keep the thing in my grasp in the first place, as soon as I lose my hold, I fall backward onto the ground.

Mustard comes to my side and licks my face, just to see if I'm all right. "Thanks, Musty; I'm fine," I say, scratching his chin. "Let's go get that darn thing back."

Immediately, my dog does a leap that looks much like a rabbit hop, from me to the base of the tree whose branches the umbrella is now entangled in. Without waiting for me to rise, Mustard starts digging a hole.

"No, no, silly dog. We need to climb up, not dig down."

He completely ignores me as he continues to dig.

"What is it, boy?" I ask, crawling toward him.

His paws become more frantic and soil goes flying everywhere, but still I have no idea what he sees. At times like these, I usually pull out my night vision goggles, but in the light of day, they won't be much use. The backpack I carry holds many useful things, but as I reach inside, I'm not entirely sure what my fingers will touch. Naturally it's a pile of granola bars and other snacks that I have to sift through first, but once my hand touches the cloth at the bottom, the real search begins.

My brain flashes an image before my hand finds the object it seeks.

About two months ago, my teacher stood in front of the class wearing plastic glasses that looked like cheap Ray Ban knock-offs with defective lenses. While the rest of the class laughed, he remained straight-faced and serious. It's a day I'll never forget for three reasons. One, Mr. Stark now knew what it felt like to be me; I'm always laughed at by large groups of students. Two, he became the coolest person I knew. And three, those glasses became an important staple in my life.

It was a lesson on pinhole glasses, a set of shades with opaque lenses perforated with tiny holes. Because of the way the light enters each hole, it increases the "depth of field" while reducing the "circle of confusion" – I could still hear Mr. Stark's voice in my head. The lesson was memorable for everyone, I think. Five pairs of pinhole glasses like the teacher wore were passed around the room, giving each of us the opportunity to see what they looked like.

While some students continued to laugh, others, like myself, took the assignment seriously. For me, they worked better than expected. There was a difference in how the light looked in certain places, shinier almost, like the glowing ring around a light bulb in a dark room. That shiny light highlighted magical elements, and I thought I spotted the glitter of fairy wings near the window. Before approaching, I checked to see if the other four students wearing glasses could see it as well, but nobody was observing that direction. When I looked back to the window, the shine was gone, and the teacher asked us to pass the glasses to the next person.

The assignment was to replicate the glasses using cardboard and construction paper, making the tenth grade science class feel more like primary school art. Regardless of the child-like lesson, I wanted a pair of those glasses... I *needed* a pair of those glasses. Even though I got the highest mark in the class, I couldn't replicate the pair I'd worn earlier.

Long after the class had ended, I continued to try to make the perfect pair of pinhole glasses using different materials each time. Finally, I conceded defeat and brought a bagful of useless pinhole glasses to Mr. Stark one day after school.

"I'm not usually a quitter, Mr. S., but I can't seem to make my glasses work," I said as I dumped the bag onto his desk. "Where can I buy a pair like yours?"

The teacher hesitated before responding, as he sifted through the glasses. "These are incredible, Britney. You're very creative."

"Most people just say weird," I countered.

He reached for the pair of glasses I made using cut toilet paper rolls and an empty Coke bottle and put them on his face. "What, exactly, is wrong with weird?"

I couldn't help but laugh as he cocked his head to the side, yet remained straight-faced as he did the first time I saw him with the strange punctured glasses.

"That's what I ask myself too, Mr. Stark."

"Well, I'll make you a deal. You leave all these wonderful glasses with me, and I will give you a pair of mine in exchange. How does that sound?"

"Really?" I clapped my hands in excitement.

"Not good enough? Well then, how about I throw in a little extra credit marks for your hard work; does that sound fair?"

"More than fair!" Jumping up and down, it was all I could not to hug him.

"It just so happens that I leave a pair in my desk drawer." Grabbing the shoelace around his neck, he fiddled with the keys hanging from it before finding the right one and sticking it into the tiny hole of his top drawer.

This probably lasted seconds, but in my mind it had been an excruciatingly long time. Maybe he would have moved faster if he removed the defunct coke bottle pinhole glasses, but I didn't want to say that.

Finally, he handed me the glasses that he'd worn as a demonstration not so many lessons ago. Shaking his hand, I thanked him a billion times, and then wore the glasses out of the room and every day after for the next three weeks. I had hoped to catch a glimpse of fairy wings in any small corner. Though the light shined differently, there was nothing else different in the school apart from more laughter and mockery.

"Well that was a complete bust," I said to myself as I threw the glasses into my backpack. *It must have just been butterfly wings I saw that day, or maybe it was a fairy, but now it has moved on.* I could think this all I wanted to, but the truth of the matter was, my heart felt those glasses showed me something that I couldn't otherwise see, so I couldn't bring myself to throw them out, or give up on them completely.

Wrapped inside my fist, I slowly bring my special glasses out of my backpack. In all the time I spent reflecting on Mr. Stark and his pinhole lesson, my dog hadn't stopped his frantic search at the bottom of the tree.

Still not convinced that the glasses will show me what I need to see, I hesitate to put them on. When Mustard begins to whine and whinny, I realize I have nothing to lose.

Closing my eyes, I place the magical glasses on my face, tucking my ashy blonde hair behind my ears as I do. "Show me what I need to see," I whisper, more so for myself. If I don't open my heart or my mind, I know I'll never be able to see the things that are right in front of my nose.

With my breath held, I open my eyes, one eyelid at a time. Sure enough, the world becomes clearer. With the reduced 'circle of confusion', I can see things that normally aren't there – or rather, that I normally can't see.

Mustard doesn't need pinhole glasses in order to reduce his confusion. He can see perfectly. Each time he moves his paw, he kicks up a combination of dirt and what looks like blue fairy dust. The further down he gets, the brighter the dust shines.

"Stop, Musty! You'll upset the fairies!"

No sooner are the words out of my mouth, then the first roar of thunder crosses the sky.

This is no time for I-told-you-sos to the weather man; I need to figure out how to get my umbrella out of the tree and begin the trek home before the sky, or the fairies, unleash their fury.

My dog isn't so good in thunderstorms; he becomes a bit of a quivering mess. No longer digging, he paces in circles around me and then nudges my hand with his nose, as if to say 'what are you waiting for? It's time to run.'

"We can't leave without my brolly," I say in response to his silent question. Any ordinary person might leave it behind, but I'm not ordinary. First of all, I'm not about to leave favourite umbrella dangling in a tree. Not only does it match my outfit – I also need it to help me on my magical quests. Plus, if I leave it behind and the fairies find it, I risk having them follow me home. Or worse, they might place a curse on it.

"I'm not about to lose my magical compass, Mustard. You know how helpful it's been in pointing out magic." I pause to scratch behind his ear, hoping to soothe him. "And you don't want the fairies finding out who we are and cursing us to a lifetime of dampness, do you?"

Hearing the sounds of raindrops as they hit the treetops, I know we're running out of time. It won't be long before the storm penetrates The Enchanted Forest. It's a well-known fact that creatures lurk in the dark; it's a lesser-known fact that dark creatures come out to play during the storms. I've heard the stories from the animals; even *they* are afraid of what goes bump in the rain.

Afraid of being captured by something wicked, I scramble to find footholds in the tree. I'm an excellent tree-climber; I just have a small fear of heights. The lowest branch has got to be about fifteen feet high, there's no way I can reach it – even Ginger Bean couldn't, and she's like seven feet tall. Sure, I might be exaggerating a little, but 'Bean' is short for 'Beanstalk' – the woman is a giant.

"We'll have to be more creative, boy, because we sure can't leave without it. Do you want to be cursed by the fairies?"

Mustard barks once as he continues to pace in circles.

23

"Well, they might not curse us, but I don't want to risk it."

Lightning flashes, lighting up the sky, and a bolt cracks loudly, striking a tree somewhere nearby… or at least that's what it sounds like.

"Death by thunderstorm, or cursed by fairies? Which is the lesser of two evils?"

Mustard responds by nudging my thigh with his snout. He then presses his body against my leg, telling me that he's going to support my choice no matter what, but also, that he's too afraid to leave my side. I need to decide quickly.

The next time the sky lights up, I notice the fairy dust that Mustard had kicked up at the base of the tree.

"That's it!" I yell in excitement.

Unsure of how it works, but trusting my gut, I grab a fistful of soil mixed with dust and close my eyes behind the shade of the pinhole glasses.

Please let this work. I just want my umbrella back.

Opening my eyes and my fingers simultaneously, I blow the dust and the dirt into the air while looking directly at the umbrella lodged several branches above.

Like magic, the fairy dust begins to sparkle brighter than the lightning had made the sky. A gust of wind picks up the dust and carries it to my umbrella, which begins to shake unnaturally as it dislodges from the tree.

At a painfully slow speed, the umbrella falls gracefully, not understanding the urgency with which I need it. The moment it's within arm's reach, I jump for it, and grip the handle tightly.

"Thank you!" I call to the elements, before turning to Mustard and yelling, "Run!" just as the next crash of thunder hits the sky.

Once the rain breaks through the treetops, it becomes difficult to see. With the high winds, it's also hard to hold my umbrella over my head and gain speed, not wanting to risk having my brolly flip inside out. Being the rocket scientist that I am, I deduce that three things need to happen, and they all need to happen now. The once helpful pinhole glasses are now obstructing my view; I take them off and tuck them into the pocket of my raincoat. The umbrella, though keeping me dry, is holding me back; with a yank and a thrust, I collapse the polka dot hindrance, and shove the hook handle into my belt loop. Before any more rain can drench my head, I pull on my large, piglet-eared hood, and try to keep it out of my eyes as I resume my fast speed pace with my dog.

If it weren't for Mustard and his wonderful sense of direction, I'm sure I'd have lost my way home. Once we cross the tree line and exit The Enchanted Forest, Mustard and I stop dead in our tracks.

There's not a cloud in the sky, and the sun is shining brightly.

"What happened to the storm?" Pulling off my hood, I look to my dog for the answer.

Not only is it a warm summer day, but there isn't a puddle anywhere on the street. It's like the city beyond the forest never saw a drop of water. Chancing a glance back to the trees, I see that there is nothing but sun's raising breaking through the leaves – like it never rained there either.

My clothes and my wet dog tell a different tale. We are soaked from head to toe.

"Ginger Bean is not going to be pleased."

I won't be able to explain to her why we're in the condition we are; I can barely explain it to myself. The only conclusion I have is that we must have stepped too close to the Blue

Fairy, and she wanted to be alone.

"Next time, Musty, we'll have to tread carefully. Don't go digging holes or kicking up magical dust without at least saying hello first."

Mustard barks once in acknowledgement before leading me the rest of the way home.

Britney Fairweather and the Dark Cloud

Today's assignment for my extracurricular photography class is to walk out into the field behind the Hallington Heights High School and snap pictures of whatever inspires us. Whether it be a twig, a leaf, or a piece of litter, we need to find a way to capture the image so that others will be able to see the inspiration in the photo.

For the six others in my after school group, the natural go-to is the rose bush that lines the fence. Amateurs. Hopeless, uninspired, unimaginative, uncreative amateurs! Being known for my originality and marching to the beat of my own drum, I, Britney Fairweather, vow to take a different course of action. Turning my back on the others, I walk in the opposite direction into the field of nothingness.

There's not so much as a dandelion for me to snap, but that's perfectly okay as my heart is just not into flowers today. The further I walk away from the roses and the group of unoriginal teens, the less I see. There's one circular patch of dead grass amongst an otherwise healthy lawn, so I snap a picture of that. Not really inspiring though, I continue onwards.

Adjusting my lens and other fun digital SLR camera settings, I rapidly photograph things in motion: a plastic bag floating in the wind, a bird flapping its wings to gain height, I even pick up and drop a helicopter leaf and snap multiple shots as it twirls back to the ground.

Chancing a glance back at the others, I hope to see if they're having better luck. Their photos, if processed correctly, will likely be beautiful. But beautiful isn't enough for me. Those roses even have the perfect backdrop of sunshine and shade to highlight all the right contours and shapes. I have a dark cloud over my head, preventing me from playing with the light in such a way. It's dark or darker for me.

Looking up to the sky just to curse it for being so mean, I realize that quite literally, I have a dark cloud over my head. It's about ten feet in circumference and looks like it's about to strike me dead with lightning.

"Sorry, Mr. Cloud!" I shout, waving my hands frantically as if to get its attention. "I'm usually a big fan of rain, but I didn't wear my favourite yellow polka dot boots today!"

The other students shake their heads and snicker in dismay, but otherwise they ignore me – as per usual.

"If you part, just a little," I continue my one-sided discussion with the cloud, "maybe a little sunshine will peep through, and I'll be able to get a good shot of light versus dark. What do you say?"

The already dark cloud turns black and cackles loudly in a thunderous roar. I've clearly offended it with my suggestion to part. Before it has the opportunity to strike me with its bolt of energy, I run like the wind out of its path.

Fortunately, it misses me, but it doesn't give up on its relentless pursuit. Never in my life has a black cloud hovered over my head, the way this one is. Figuratively, maybe, but not literally. It doesn't matter how hard I try to dodge the cloud, it continues to follow. Dashing to the right, and then again to the left, I zigzag as much as possible, but still, I can't shake it.

"Fine!" I yell. "No sunshine for me. I get it!" Like an old man, I shake my fist at the sky. If it's going to strike me with lightning, let it.

Then I get the genius idea to lie on the ground and point my camera at the cloud. How cool would it be if I got a picture of lightning as it came toward me? Sure I might die, but I'd be legendary.

"Bring it, Mr. Cloud. I can handle you."

As I wait for death, I begin to snap photos. Another rumble from the sky, though not as furious as before, tells me that the cloud is amused. Not only does it lighten to a paler shade of black, almost grey but not quite, it also breaks open just a tad, and out pops the thinnest ray of sunshine.

I must have taken over a dozen photos from as many angles as I could get without actually moving my body, lest I inadvertently offend Mr. Cloud again. Just when I am about ready to call it a day, one single drop of rain comes flying toward me at high speed. I rapidly click my button again before moving the camera out of the way. I'm not as fortunate as the drop smacks me directly in the middle of my forehead, but c'est la vie; it's only rain.

Normally, I'd challenge the sky with a line about that being the best it could do, but given the expensive equipment in my hands, I decide it best to keep my mouth shut. Standing up and readying myself to take cover, I look up one final time. It's the polite thing to do, to thank the cloud for giving me such amazing shots. To my surprise, however, the cloud is gone. I am now standing in an open field, on a very sunny day.

It may have been all part of my elaborate imagination, but

the little drop of rain still remaining on my forehead says otherwise... I guess we'll see how the photos turn out; either way, I'm inspired.

Britney Fairweather and the Cure for Mustard

The swing in my backyard needs no pushing. Every time I sit on the plastic seat, rain or shine, summer or winter, I start to sway. That sway soon becomes a full on push/pull without any help from my legs. Even on days when there is absolutely no wind, I can still pick up a great speed, reaching as high as the linked chain will allow. This only happens for me. I've seen Ginger Bean, also known as 'Mom', sit on the swing from time to time, and it doesn't move for her. When I sit on the swing, I have to dig my heels into the grass below in order to stop my movement.

After fifteen years, and all the weird things that happen to or around me, I no longer ask why this happens, but rather, why does a teenager still have a swing set in her backyard? Due to its oddities and possible magic, I never asked my mother to get rid of it, but I find it strange that she hasn't tossed it out one day while I'm at school. Each day I come home wondering if it'll be gone, and each day I'm surprised that it's still here. At what age does a parent think their child has outgrown a swing set?

It's a great play set though, and I'm grateful I still have it. All those times that I was grounded for going too far into the woods behind my house, or not coming straight home after school, I was at least allowed in the backyard. And on beautiful summer days, like today, when I'm home alone with nothing to do, a swing in the backyard is great to have. A magical swing that requires no effort is even better.

I try to test the strength of the magic by swaying against its current path. With all my weight, I rock side to side when it moves back and forth. When I think I'm in control, that I've beaten the magic and am guiding the swing where I want it to go, left to right, right to left, I stop applying pressure and expect to slow to a stop. After a few good minutes, I realize the magic has taken over, and there's no need to swing myself. Again I try to fight the force, and after some time, I'm successful.

"Take that magic swing!" I say to no one in particular.

Sure enough, the swing stops dead in its tracks, and since it's on the upswing, I end up flying through the air and landing on my face in the dirt. "Touché."

No more playing with magic for me. I roll over and lie on my back, basking in the sun while I collect my thoughts. It's then I remember why I came outside in the first place. The magic swing distracted me.

Needing another distraction, I decide to go on a witch-hunt. Normally I bring my dog, Mustard, for these types of adventures, but he's on his way to the vet with Ginger Bean. It's only his annual shot, but I find myself worrying anyway, which is what led me to the backyard in the first place.

Mustard doesn't like needles; he'll no doubt have a panic attack. I should be there; I shouldn't have let my mother talk me out of going.

"You'll only stress him out more, Britney. He'll see you on edge, and then he'll be upset."

At the time, I believed her, but now I'm not so sure. While staring at the clouds, I thought up a plan to help Mustard. Surely a witch will be able to cast a spell to help relieve my dog's pain. Maybe if she's nice enough, she'll create another potion that we can both take beforehand, something to ease our nerves – that way we'll both be calm come needle time.

After running back in the house and arming myself with a backpack full of witch-hunt materials and snacks, I am ready to go. Decked out in my favourite yellow polka dot rain boots, despite the lack of rain, I trek out my kitchen door, across my lawn, past the swing set, beyond the gate, and into the woods I call 'The Enchanted Forest.'

Although there is reason to wear the boots: the forest is always full of mud; I can't get away with carrying an umbrella. Should anyone happen to see me out and about, they'd think I was crazy. I get that enough at school; I don't need it during my summer holiday as well.

Normally, I carry my matching yellow polka dot umbrella with me on all my adventures, as it's a good indicator of magic. It was a hard decision to make, leaving the umbrella at home. There's no way I can find a witch without a tool to point me in the right direction. *Think, Britney, think. What can I use to point me in the direction of a witch who is no doubt hidden in the realms of her magic?*

Nearly tripping over a large stick buried underneath some leaves, I figure that's my subconscious answering my otherwise rhetorical question. The stick is longer and heavier than I expect it to be when I pick it up.

My natural reaction is to look upward to the branches still attached to the large trees. "Are you okay, Mr. Oak?" I ask, placing a palm on the nearest trunk. "You're missing a limb!"

The leaves shake in the wind, and it appears as though the

tree is laughing at me.

"Well, if you don't need it, do you mind if I take it? I'm hoping it'll direct me to the Good Witch of the Woods." I know there are more witches, but in The Enchanted Forest, there is only one known for her kindness – and she's not always kind.

The breeze blows gently, again ruffling the leaves high above, and I take this as consent.

"Thank you, Mr. Oak!"

The branch in my hands is heavier than my preferred type of magic wand, so I squeeze the base with both fists. "We can do this," I say, more so to myself.

Once the branch is pointed northward, I begin my walk deeper into the forest, away from the path. A long time passes before I wonder when the branch will lead me in a new direction. Just as I'm about to pause for a break, a tiny little leaf grows on the tip of the right side of my compass.

"East it is," I say, taking steps to the right. "Thank you kindly." I stroke the base of the branch so it knows I'm appreciative. Since I'm putting all my faith into this as a compass, I need it to know that I am grateful. Otherwise it might lead me astray, or worse, to one of the bad witches.

After several steps eastbound, a second leaf grows beside the first. Since I can't go any more east, I turn only slightly before continuing my trek. As I walk, I begin to wonder how Mustard is at the vet's. *Has he had his needle yet? Did it hurt?*

"Don't worry, Musty; I'll find you a cure!"

The branch in my hands can feel my urgency. Simultaneously, three new leaves grow on the left. Following its guidance, I'm led around a birdbath.

"Odd. Why is there a birdbath in the middle of the woods? I've never noticed this before." The little hairs on my arms stand on edge as I realize I haven't heard, or seen, any birds in the last few minutes. It's deadly silent.

In one magical moment, all of the newly grown leaves on my guiding stick disappear as they get sucked back into the branch itself. My hands begin to tremble around the piece of wood, and I wonder if it is the branch's fear that I'm feeling.

My natural reaction is to soothe the branch, but something tells me I need to remain quiet. Ducking behind a big tree, I count to five to gather some courage and settle my nerves. Peering around the thick trunk, I look for clues.

Something is close; I can smell it.

There is something in the air; my nose realizes this before my brain does. It's not intuition; I can very clearly smell smoke. Surely I would have realized if there was a forest fire. The branch had been kind to me, its father laughed with me, and I followed all of the proper etiquette rules when dealing with matter from The Enchanted Forest. I may be naïve sometimes, but I really doubt the magical compass led me to danger.

Looking up through the leaves above, I have to squint to see the sky. There is something near, I know it – and it's not a forest fire; I would have felt the heat and seen the endless amount of orange. It's not black smoke either – in fact, it's purple.

The sky was what gave me the answer. Midday in the summer, I should have seen flecks of blue between the leaves, but instead, all I see are thick purple clouds.

"Aha! That's where the smell is coming from. Purple smoke means potion making. The witch must be near her cauldron."

Expecting silence as a response, since I'm more or less speaking to myself, I am shocked when I hear cackling. Right when I'm about to comment on the cliché of it all, the cackle turns into a cough, a horrible, relentless, dry cough.

Please be the Good Witch of the Woods; please be the Good Witch of the Woods, I chant to myself. With fingers crossed, I hope that, whoever she is, she's in a good mood.

"Are you okay?" I ask, not seeing the witch but assuming she's nearby.

"Who goes there?" the raspy voice calls in return.

"Britney Fairweather, Hallington Heights High School Student. Who am I speaking with?" I learned from other creatures of The Enchanted Forest that it's best to introduce one's self with name and title. I don't exactly have a title, so I'm hoping 'student' is enough.

A thick cloud of purple smoke appears before me. My nostrils flare as my throat closes. Waving my hands frantically, attempting to clear the smoke, I close my eyes as they begin to tear. Naturally, I start to cough as well, and it sounds a lot like the witch's cough from before.

When I'm able to breathe, I sneak a peek at the cloud in front of me and notice that it has disappeared. In its place stands the witch, who is taller than I expect her to be. If I had to guess, I'd say she is easily over six feet tall. Her clothes are baggy, but even still, it's evident that the witch is quite thin. If she has any weight to her at all, it is largely due to the volume of hair she possesses. Thick violet dreadlocks sit heavily down the length of her back. Maybe I had some cliché expectations of how she'd look, so I'm surprised that she's covered from head to toe in purple and sparkly silver.

Her beautiful, floor-length gown with a train that drags in the leaves is covered with silver sequins that shine in the sun.

As she takes a step toward me, I can make out her shoes, silver stilettos to match her gown. Getting a glimpse of the long, thin spike of the heel, I now understand why she appears so tall. What I don't understand is how she is so clean. The bottom of her dress should be covered with mud, and her heels should be sinking into the earth with each of her steps.

Except, the woman is immaculate. Everything about her is pristine, right down to the jewels. Rings, bracelet, necklace, and earrings, all a matching set of sparkly purple gems. They're too dark to be amethyst; this is a stone I've never seen. Inside the pear-shaped charm that hangs from a thin silver chain around her neck, I see something that catches my eye. It reminds me of a galaxy, the way it swirls and glows, flecked with tiny stars. I could stare at this jewel for hours; I already find myself getting lost in it.

When I see movement at the corner of my eye, I snap back to reality. The witch hadn't taken any more steps toward me, so what was it that caught my eye? I wait a moment before addressing the woman, wondering if she's placed me under a spell. That brief pause gives me time to see what I had missed before: her dreadlocks. Sure, I'd noticed their length and thickness, and the fact that they were as purple as the trinkets she wears, but I hadn't noticed the way they move.

In the heart of The Enchanted Forest, cloaked in trees so tall you can barely see the sky, there is no chance of wind, or even a gentle breeze. The witch's snake-like hair moves all on its own. The longer I stare, the more it comes to life. This time, I shake off the trance, not wanting to be hypnotized by the Good Witch of the Woods. At this point, I'm still only guessing that's who she is.

Raising my eyes, I have to tilt back my head to get a good look at hers. The way she cackles makes me think she'll have green skin and a pointy black hat. With the exception of her hair, she could easily stand in for a Disney Princess. Pale skin with rose-coloured cheeks, eyes purple as the smoke from before, framed by the longest eyelashes I've ever seen, this woman could possibly be the most beautiful creature of the woods.

"You will forget my name before you leave here, Britney Fairweather of Hallington Heights High. There is no point to me giving it." The witch interrupts my mental assessment of her, answering the question I forgot that I asked.

"Fair enough, Ma'am. I mean no disrespect. Are you the Good Witch of the Woods?" It may seem like a redundant question, I know full well that she's a witch, and she's very clearly in the woods, but this is the only way I can find out if her intentions are to harm, or not to.

"My intentions are none of your concern, child."

It doesn't take a genius to know that she can read thoughts. Very quickly I begin to picture Mustard and all the pain he's probably feeling right this second. "Please, Ma'am, I need your help."

The witch nods ever so slightly, and I truly hope this is her way of showing that she will tend to my needs.

"I don't much care for the needs of humans; they never match my own."

Before I can beg her to change her mind, she silences me by raising her hand. That slight gesture is no doubt the casting of a spell, as I literally cannot open my mouth to say a single word. A single tear falls from the corner of my eye as I picture my dog suffering and scared, helpless to the vet who will soon prick him.

Just then, the witch's hair moves again, all on its own.

I think her dreads are coming to life, but the cause of the movement makes itself known. A large brown rat comes out from behind her neck, and sits on her shoulder, scowling at me.

The witch's voice softens. "I, too, have a four-legged furry friend. Marble here would be terrified to receive such treatment, and I would do my best to soothe him. I believe I can help you, young Britney Fairweather. Follow me, and keep your hands to yourself. If anything should happen, I will curse you to a life full of warts."

"Yes, Ma'am," I say feeling small, only slightly relieved that my voice has returned.

I want very much to bring my magical compass with me, lest I get lost on the return trip, but the witch will probably assume that I'll use the branch as a weapon, and she may cast her spell against me. To the branch, I whisper, "I can't bring you with me. You are too big. Be safe, and I will find you again."

The stick cowers in my hands, and I really don't want to let it go. It was careless of me to bring it so far from its home, with no intent to return it. "I will find a way, I promise," I soothe the branch. While I run my thumb over its base, the witch gets further away from me. I need to run to catch up; I have no time to feel remorse over the fallen oak limb. Just as I am about to drop it, the branch grows smaller and smaller until it is no more the size of a twig.

"Thank you," I whisper as I place it into my pocket and begin to jog to keep step with the lady ahead.

The witch picks up speed, and I struggle to follow. She laces her way through many trees, and right when I think I'm caught up, she disappears completely. Resisting the urge to stamp my foot and cry out in temper-tantrum fashion, I stop abruptly and wait for her return.

Sure enough, the massive tree to my left opens, showing me a dark hole that I am too afraid to enter.

"Come in, if you dare, child," the witch beckons from the hollow.

"I dare not, I don't have my night vision with me today," I call in response. The witch's evil laugh cackles from the depths of the hole. "If it means my dog's safety and comfort," I continue, "I'll follow you blindly."

Two very purple eyes can be seen in the darkness of the tree. These eyes appear to change shape, multiply, and then in a blink, return to the original shape. Out steps the witch, and as soon as she is fully above ground, the tree's magical hollow begins to close.

"I was teasing, child. We can stay outside where it's safe. I just needed to collect some herbs from my stash. Are you ready to chant with me?"

Exhaling, I say, "Yes, Ma'am," relieved that I don't have to go underground.

With a flick of the witch's hand, another burst of smoke appears. It starts as the purple I recognized from before, but quickly turns from that to green, to red, and then weirdly enough, the red smoke turns to water and falls from the air, landing in the cauldron that magically appears below it.

"Cool trick, I wish I could do stuff like that," I mutter.

The lady rolls her eyes as her pet rat makes his way out of hiding, taking its place on her shoulder once more. The Good Witch pulls out an assortment of herbs, plants, and something that looks like dryer lint from a satchel I hadn't noticed before, and casts them into her brewing pot. Whatever it is, the dryer lint causes the thick liquid to begin to boil, bubbling to the top and sizzling over the edge.

The witch cackles maniacally before beginning her chant. The language is foreign to me, and while I'd like to be able to join in, I really can't. It is smarter for me to wait to be told, I don't want to break her focus or inadvertently change the effects of the potion she is making for my dog.

Her chanting continues, increasing in volume, but I hear a softer voice in my head. It's very clearly the witch's voice, and not my own thoughts, but as I stare at the woman, her focus remains on the bubbling cauldron and her foreign chant.

"I want you to think of your furry pet, Britney Fairweather. Picture his happiness. Picture his favourite thing to do, his favourite thing to eat, his favourite thing to see. Let this be the only thing you think about as you repeat the words: Pain begone."

Happy images of Mustard dance around my head: him sitting, silently begging for food with his tongue hanging out of his mouth and his tail sliding back and forth on the floor; him rolling all over my mother's bed, messing up her perfectly pristine duvet when he knows that he's not allowed to be up there; him running around The Enchanted Forest with me on strange quests to find mythical creatures; and then lying in bed beside me at night, waiting for me to cuddle him.

When the witch tells me to, I begin to chant, "Pain begone, pain begone, pain begone…"

The voice in my head says to close my eyes and continue chanting, so I do. I'm not religious, but I kind of hoped it would be more like Hail Marys – like the witch would tell me to chant seven times and my dog would be cured. There seems to be no end; the words are beginning to lose meaning for me as they mush into a string of syllables, painbegonepainbegonepainbegone, pain beg on? *Focus, Britney*!

Saying the words stupidly might cause my dog more pain. "Pain begone!" I snap myself back to attention and repeat the words with more emphasis and crisper phonetics.

The witch chants something loud enough to override my thoughts, but speaks to me mentally to say something else. Before I can grasp how she's speaking two different languages simultaneously, the voice in my head says, "Almost done. Keep chanting. When you see your dog, give him one dose of the vial while petting him gently. Soothe him the way you normally would, and the potion will go down easily. Pain begone. Pain begone. Pain begone…"

I repeat the words with the witch long after I stop hearing her voice in my head. It soon dawns on me that I can't hear her weird language outside my head, either. In the depths of the forest, there's nothing but silence and my two-word chant. When the realization hits, my mouth shuts, and my eyes snap open on their own accord. There I stand, alone in the woods… no witch, no rat, no cauldron, and no colour-changing smoke. Even the twig that I had pocketed before, has returned to its full-grown original state, and is now held tightly within my grasp. The birdbath is back in its odd place. *This is a trap,* I think. There are no birds in the area because, should they choose to bathe or drink from the marble sculpture, they'd probably be turned into the next potion ingredient for the ballroom witch.

Shaking off the scary thought, I ask, "What happened?" knowing the stick couldn't answer. It appears as though nothing has happened… like nothing ever happened. There's no trace of the events that led me to this particular spot in the woods. Even the tree that opened into a burrow for the witch to store her herbs is no longer there.

"Thank you, Lady Witch!" I call to the vacant forest.

Scanning the ground in an effort to find the vial of potion proves fruitless. Well, not entirely fruitless, I do manage to find an apple core. Not too many people travel through the forest, and when they do, they stick to the path. Since I'm too deep in the woods that even I can't find my way back to the trails, I deduce that the apple core has to be from the cauldron; it hasn't even begun to rot yet. Either the rest of the apple was an ingredient of the spell, or the witch happened to snack while I was busy chanting.

Picking up litter is something I do without being told, but compost is good for the earth, so I leave it alone and begin looking for the supposed vial. If it wasn't for the apple core, I could probably convince myself that both the sparkly witch and her snarling rat were products of my imagination.

"Why the heck did I bother with the chanting if we weren't making a pain-reliever for my dog?" I ask my compass, as I wave it around hoping it'll have better luck in the search.

The stick in my hand grows two small leaves on either side, giving it the appearance of a shrug.

"Will you guide me home, wooden friend? I need to get back before Mustard does. I want to be the first thing he sees when he runs through the door."

As the two little leaves are sucked back into the thick branch, one large leaf grows from the tip, and I know I need to walk straight ahead. As I walk, I continue to look for the potion, not yet ready to give up on the idea of its existence. Every once in a while I peer up at the tip of the stick to make sure that I'm still going in the right direction. With each step away from the chanting spot, dread and disappointment fill my heart.

Not only did I waste my day looking for a cure instead of waiting at home for Mustard's return from the vet, but I don't even have a magic potion to ease his nerves and relieve his pain. Why would the witch lie to me? Why would she make me do all that chanting? What was the point of all that purple smoke? Why bother?

Just as I'm beginning to feel tears forming in my eyes, I find myself at the path and no longer need the branch's guidance. I run the rest of the way home, stopping only to return my magical compass to the tall oak tree. My vision begins to blur, and I know that I've started to cry. If I run faster, I wonder, maybe it'll make the pain in my heart and the stinging in my eyes disappear.

"You'll be okay, Mustard! I'm coming!" I call out, more to motivate myself to continue the marathon sprint.

Soon enough, I reach my back fence. To save time, I climb the fence instead of opening the gate. This normally wouldn't save time, but at the speed I was going, I was able to leap nearly to the top. With a strong grip and a swing of my feet, I am over the wire fence and landing carelessly on my lawn in three swift moves.

Making a mental note to try that method again, I dash for my backdoor and storm into the kitchen, forgetting to kick off my favourite rubber boots. I realize quickly that I've traipsed mud all over Ginger Bean's sparkling, clean linoleum.

"Mom will be so upset, if she comes home to see this dirty mess!" I say to myself.

After kicking off the boots and placing them gently on the mat beside the door, I grab some paper towel from the countertop, dip it in water, and get down on my hands and knees in order to clean the mess I had just made. It takes quite a few paper towels and plenty of muscle to scrub out all of the mud, and when I am done, the kitchen floor is nowhere near back to the spotless condition I found it in.

How does she get it so clean? We keep our mop and bucket in our laundry room, but I'm not sure if I have enough time to do any more cleaning before Mom and Mustard return from the vet's. Sometimes Ginger takes him to the dog park, but usually she tells me first so that I can go too. *Maybe she's running errands? She really should be here by now.*

"Oh well, worst case scenario, they come home to find me cleaning the floors; best case scenario, they come home to clean floors, and Mom doesn't need to know about my muddy mess.

After filling the bucket with warm water, I add a capful of floor cleaner and ring out the mop head. It was wet before I started, so I figure that Mom must have just cleaned the floor this morning. *No wonder it was so shiny.*

I start to mop the spot in front of the door first and continue along all the spots that I had walked on before removing my boots. Considering I cleaned it up with paper towel first, there's really no trace. I'm mopping for the shine factor. It works too, except now there's a sparkly clean path in the middle of the room, but the rest of the floor is lacking the lustre.

"Alright, Britney, you're not being practical," I say to myself as I make my way to the far corner of the kitchen. "Start here, and end at the laundry room. I can do this."

It takes longer than it probably should, but I'm extra thorough. I walk backwards as I mop the floor in front of me, going over everything twice, and three times over corners and crevices. Once I've mopped myself through the kitchen and into the laundry room, I realize I'm stuck with the mop and bucket full of dirty water. Hopping up onto the washing machine, I clean the last section of floor then ring out the mop and carefully empty the bucket into the laundry sink. Now all I have to do is sit here until the floor dries.

Counting out loud to pass the time, I get to one hundred and sixty-seven when I hear Mom's car pull into the driveway. I leap from the washer, dash to the door, and attempt to run across the kitchen to the entrance to the living room, when I hit a wet spot and slide along the floor. I'm not as graceful as they make it seem in the movies, and I fall on my butt... painfully.

As I struggle to stand, Mustard runs in, tongue hanging from his mouth. "Hey, boy! How you feeling?" I wince, knowing he probably feels worse than me.

Mustard licks a long line up my cheek, but that doesn't soothe my nerves. "You can tell me the truth, buddy. Did it hurt?"

I scratch the sweet spot just behind his ear, and he begins thumping his leg on the floor to the same rhythm. If that isn't clue enough, he rolls over on my lap, belly up, and closes his eyes. "You want bellies, Mustard?"

'Bellies' is what we in the Fairweather household call the famous belly rub. If done correctly, Mustard can be put right to sleep, face up, all stretched out, on the floor of whatever room we leave him in.

As I frantically scratch behind his ear with one hand, and rub his tummy gently with the other, I mentally chant, "Pain begone, pain begone, pain begone."

In only a few moments, I hear the comforting sounds of my dog snoring.

"Thank you, Good Witch of the Woods," I whisper under my breath.

Britney Fairweather and the Bottomless Puddle

My dog and I like to splash in puddles, but deep in The Enchanted Forest, puddles aren't always what they seem.

While hopping through puddles and chasing my dog, Mustard, between trees beyond my backyard fence, I come across a large pond that seems too big to have been created by the day's rain.

"It's just one big puddle, boy. We can jump in it like any other."

Except it wasn't… and we couldn't. Somehow, I find myself at the bottom of a marsh when only moments before I was on a dirt path in the woods.

Kicking and flailing around doesn't get me any closer to the water's surface. Just when I'm about to panic, I see a spark as it approaches me from the near distance. Little by little, the dot grows into a ball and begins to take shape. Soon I can see two tiny little legs with feet that come to sharp points.

A water sprite!

"Yes," the sprite replies. I can hear the tinny voice as clear in my mind as if I thought the word myself.

"Respectfully, Ms. Sprite, I need oxygen," I think, hoping she can hear me in her head as easily as I could hear her in

mine.

"Breathe, young child. I have given you a gift," she says through the water and not telepathically, as she swims into view.

I can make out every detail. It's as if she emits the ball of light to surround us both. Not only can I see everything clearly, but I feel dry, warm, and above water. The gift must be to breathe under water using her magical orb of light.

Testing the theory, I say to her, "Thank you…" I want to say more, but I'm shocked that I'm able to speak at all. I should have swallowed water and drowned. Before thinking myself into a panic attack, I focus on the little creature's attributes.

She looks a lot like I'd expect a fairy to look; standing no more than three inches tall, pointed features, olive skin, yellow eyes and rosy cheeks. Her clothing appears to be made from a red maple leaf, wrapped around her body, toga-style.

"What is your name?" I ask as politely as possible, trying not to stare at her wild blue hair, as it seems to take on a life of its own.

"I am Sapphire."

"Nice to meet you, Sapphire," I say, extending my hand for her to shake. "I am—"

"I know who you are, child!" Her hair grows longer, and I'm reminded of Medusa. I hope it doesn't turn to snakes, but nothing would surprise me. It's clear by Sapphire's now amber eyes that she is angry with me.

I know better than to upset a water sprite. If she ends her spell, the orb will break, and I'll be stuck under water in a marsh that no one else will be able to find. In situations like these, it's best to say nothing at all. So I wait, and watch as her hair grows and shrinks depending on her mood. When it's a touch shorter, I know she's calming. Her amber eyes fade back to their original yellow.

"You are Britney Fairweather, Child Who Sees."

"Yes, Ma'am, that's me. But I'm not really a child, I'm fifteen now."

"Silence!" Her voice sounds like bells and whistles, but the command makes the little hairs on the back of my neck stand to attention. "Why have you come?" she asks, eyes calm, but hair beginning to grow.

"I was just taking my dog for a walk, honest. We like to look for adventures."

"Your dog?"

"The four-legged furry thing currently sniffing around the water's edge. I call him Mustard. He's a great companion... understands me better than anyone else on the planet." I tend to ramble when I'm nervous. Normally that doesn't bother me, but in the presence of a water sprite who holds the fate of my life in her hands, it's something I'm consciously trying to stop.

"The beast is your companion? Your mate?" Sapphire is both shocked and holding back a laugh. With her in a better mood, I feel slightly safer. I don't want to correct her, but it's best not to lie.

"He's my pet, and he's not a beast, just a big, hairy, drooling machine."

"Pet?"

Do water sprites have some sort of pet? Tree nymphs are said to ride birds, I wonder if the sprites do something similar.

"What about frogs? Do you speak with frogs at all?" I ask.

"Speak? No, not like this. The frogs are our friends. We can communicate with them, but not by words."

"That's kind of like my dog. He understands the words I say to him, but he doesn't use words when speaking to me."

"I've tried speaking to that *thing* before. He didn't understand at all!"

I giggle just a little bit. "Mustard understands better than most dogs. Next time you speak to him, try saying only one or two words at a time. If you scratch him behind the ear, he'll pretty much do anything you want."

Sapphire opens her mouth to speak, but before any words come out, Mustard begins to howl so loud that I can hear him inside the orb.

The little sprite covers both her ears with her hands. "Why is he making that insufferable noise?"

"He's worried about me. I need to be on land. Sapphire, I appreciate the gift of… of breathing under water… and of allowing me to speak with you… but I really need to go. Can we talk up there on the ground for a little while? I'm sure I don't need to be home right away, I just need to pat Mustard on the head and tell him I'm okay."

"You are free to go, child. As long as that beast is about, we will remain hidden." At the mention of 'we' half a dozen little white sparks flashed, followed by another dozen, and another. When the entire bottom of the marsh is lit with a brilliant white glow, I have to shield my eyes. The glare seeps through my fingers and I can no longer count the amount of water sprites in the pond. I close my eyes tightly, and within seconds the glare is gone, leaving me in nothing but darkness. Opening my eyes in a panic, I realize too quickly that all the sprites are gone, and so is the orb. I swim to the top with ease, and call for my dog.

Mustard licks the mud from my face as I crawl out of the marsh. He goes eerily quiet as I squeeze the water from my clothing. When he begins to pant, I turn my attention to him. A tiny ball of white light is sitting just behind his right ear. Sapphire, or one of the other water sprites, is scratching his sweet spot.

"I told you, he's harmless," I whisper loud enough I hope the sprite can hear me, but not so loud I startle Mustard into realizing it's not me scratching his ear.

The spark flashes twice and disappears.

"Come on, boy. We better go now. Mom will be waiting."

A few steps in the direction of my house, I turn back to wave goodbye to the sprites.

To my surprise, and yet not, the marsh is gone.

Jaclyn Aurore

Britney Fairweather and the Memory Thieves

Present Day...

Ginger Bean, otherwise known as 'my mom', has been going through these weekend spurts where all she does is bake or buy ingredients for baking. I asked her once if she was miserable or lonely, to which she replied, "Don't be silly, Britney. People bake for the sheer enjoyment of it, not because they don't have anything better to do."

Truthfully, the tall redheaded woman never looks happier than she does in an apron and oven mitts. She hip-checks me out of the way as she bends over, opening the oven door once more.

"Ouch, Mom... excuse me works too."

"Honey, I'm on a tight schedule here," she says, lifting the cookie sheet from the oven, and placing another in that she had prepared already. After casting her oven mitts to the countertop, she sets the timer, and paces around the kitchen opening up every cupboard and drawer.

Following her around at least three paces behind, I resist the urge to close the things she leaves open. "Do you need help finding something?" I ask. It's obvious she does, but it's best to keep my sarcasm to myself.

"Nutmeg... I need nutmeg."

"I can't be too sure, but I don't think you'll find nutmeg in with the forks and knives." Just like that, I'd forgotten about the rule on sarcasm.

Thankfully, Ginger Bean ignores my remark and continues to scramble around the kitchen. Well if it's nutmeg she needs, I'm sure I can offer a helping hand. I get down on my hands and knees and crawl around the kitchen floor looking for the missing spice. Not knowing what he's looking for, my faithful dog, Mustard, begins to sniff around in excitement.

"It's a thin shaker with a brown powder substance in it, Musty. It's probably labelled, but you'll know it when you start sneezing." The dog continues to sniff close to the bottom of the fridge as if he understands.

Looking under the refrigerator to see if perhaps the little jar rolled underneath, I'm only slightly disappointed to see nothing but dust bunnies. The kitchen isn't very big, I've circled it twice on all fours and so has Mustard. For a moment, I picture my dog trying to scout the kitchen on just two legs. He could either balance himself on his back paws and walk around looking eye level with the kitchen counters, or maybe he'd balance himself on his front paws and walk around like a circus act... although I don't think he'd get much nutmeg-searching done.

After giggling briefly, I realize that I'm giggling to myself... where did my mother go?

As if answering my thoughts, my mom calls from the front room, "Brit, I'm running out for a quick sec. Can you please take the cookies out when the timer goes?"

Before I get a chance to respond, I hear the door slam and the engine of the car start. "Sure, Ginger," I call out to no one. "I can handle that!"

In the meantime, I continue to look for the missing nutmeg. I mean really, it's obvious that's what my mother left the house for, more nutmeg, but there must be an empty spice jar lying around somewhere... and I can't even see that. This leads me to believe that Ginger Bean misplaced it and didn't use it up.

"Or maybe she didn't misplace it," I say, looking directly at my dog who is now sitting with wagging tail, looking up at me... presumably waiting for the next command. "Maybe it was stolen!"

Mustard barks once. He gets just as excited as I do at the thought of our next adventure.

"Who do you think it could be? Nymphs? Sprites? Fairies? Pixies?" I list off all the small flying creatures first, counting each on my fingers. "Hmm, what would any of them need with nutmeg? They're not the type to cast spells or make potions... and when they do use magic, it's a natural dust."

Mustard uses his snout to nudge my hand, ending my monologue abruptly. Sitting on the floor next to him, I pat his head and continue speculating. "Trolls? No, they are allergic to nutmeg... everyone knows that... Gnomes? Well, maybe, I suppose... but not the Garden Gnomes, they've been cursed to a lifetime of immobility. The Siberian Gnomes are too far, as are the Dune Gnomes. I haven't come across any Woodland Gnomes in our Enchanted Forest, Mustard... though maybe they've just kept themselves hidden so far."

The dog, knowing he has been spoken too, licks my hand in acknowledgement, and I continue to scratch just under his chin.

"Witches, maybe… they could for sure benefit from stolen spices. But I've never seen a witch enter anyone's house without permission. They are known for stealing and tricking, but they respectfully wait before entering one's humble abode. I very much doubt any witch is the cause of our missing nutmeg."

This much thinking makes me hungry, and Mom's cookies smell delicious. After shifting Mustard's body weight off my lap and onto the floor, I make my way to the kitchen sink. I take extra care to wash my hands, partly because I have to get off all the dog fur, and partly because I love the smell of our soap. While towel drying my hands, I look around the kitchen, trying to decide which of Mom's cookies would make the best snack. She's not known for her cooking skills, but her baking abilities are superb.

According to the timer, I have four minutes to decide which cookie I want to eat prior to being distracted by the horribly loud buzzer on the oven. "Time for an inventory, Mustard. One cookie, five plates. Tough call."

I point to the plate nearest me, and tell my dog what I see. "Peanut butter, I can tell by the fork marks." We step two paces to the right, and I point to the next plate. "Very clearly chocolate chip, double chocolate chip. Sorry, boy, you can't have any of these ones."

Mustard whines just a touch, but this is not something I'll cave on. "It's for your own good, Musty. Dogs can't digest chocolate… or something. It might be an urban legend or an old wives' tale, but I'm not testing it out and risking your life. Plus Ginger Bean usually makes you homemade dog treats anyway, so all of these are for me." Spreading my hands out to show the dog I mean all five plates, I continue, "Even these shortbread cookies and ginger snaps." I can't help but laugh at the thought of Ginger Bean making ginger snaps. "Do you think she ran out of ginger, and not nutmeg? Maybe she's got her spices confused."

The far counter holds the plate of cookies I have my eye on. These are my favourite of the bunch, and the hardest to make. "Empire biscuits, also called Belgium cookies, depending on who makes them. A layer of strawberry jam sandwiched between two shortbread cookies, with a layer of vanilla icing, topped with a quarter slice of a maraschino cherry smack dab in the centre. Can't get any better than this!"

My right hand has a mind of its own as it reaches for the cookie at the top of the pile. Mustard barks once, and I remember my manners. Using my left hand, I take my right and place it in my pants' pocket. "You're right, boy. I shouldn't have the first cookie. Not without her permission at least. What was I thinking? She's not even here!"

With what little will power I have left, I make my way to the cookie jar for store bought cookies instead. There's a trick to the lid that requires two hands for lifting, so my right hand is freed from its pocket prison. One shake, rattle, and shimmy later, the lid pops off, and I'm finally able to get my sweet treat reward. Except... except, I'm not able to get anything at all. The stupid cookie jar is empty!

There's a loud growl that I'm not entirely sure is my equally empty belly, or Mustard who is just as disappointed by this discovery as I am.

"How am I supposed to have milk and cookies, with no cookies?" Pouring myself a glass, I contemplate the meaning of life... or at least a life without cookies. "If there is no cookie to dip in the milk, will the milk taste as good?"

As I'm sipping for the answer, the loud siren from the stovetop startles me out of my philosophical thoughts. Thankfully, I only need one oven mitt to remove the tray of cookies from the oven, as I can't seem to find the other.

"That's odd," I say, while turning off the blaring sound of the timer. "I know I saw Mom with two oven mitts before she dashed out the door on her nutmeg mission. Where could the other one be?"

Mustard cocks his head to the side, and I'm pretty sure that means he doesn't have the answer either.

"Let's go to the living room to regroup. I can't be around all these cookies and not be able to eat them!" I chug back the rest of my milk, hoping that will fill the void until Mom comes home, then I head to the couch, where Mustard and I can figure out what's happening.

"Okay, boy, not only is there no more nutmeg, a spice that I'm pretty sure my mother didn't use much of while baking today, but the jar that the nutmeg is kept in has disappeared as well, so has a single oven mitt, and all the store-bought cookies. I smell trickery afoot! We've deduced that it's not trolls, gnomes, fairies, pixies, nymphs, sprites, or witches..." I scratch my chin as I drift off in thought. Mustard scratches his ear with his back paw.

We both jump off the couch together as I proclaim, "Elves!" I smack my palm to my forehead. "Why didn't I think of this before? It's so obvious! House elves steal things all the time. They're nothing at all like the helpful elves in that Harry Potter series. I should know, I've caught plenty in their guilty act."

They really are silly creatures, house elves. All of their crimes are innocent, mostly just to poke fun at the homeowner. The thing they are most commonly known for doing is stealing laundry; Harry Potter got that right, though it has nothing to do with being declared independent... Wait... maybe I'm remembering Harry Potter wrong. How could they declare independence by stealing? No, no, that doesn't make sense.

It's neither here nor there really. At the end of the day, house elves are mischievous characters who steal laundry, not to wear it, but so that the owner of the clothing article is driven insane when it goes missing. Sure, it all starts small, a single sock from the dryer, a winter hat – stolen in the summer, that blouse that can only be worn with one particular skirt on special occasions that only fall on a warm but not wet spring day.

"I know you have my blouse, Elf," I call to the empty house. "But the joke is on you! I can wear that nice skirt with just about anything!" This is more of a lie, but house elves don't honour or value honesty, so no harm done.

Turning my attention back to the four-legged beast looking up at me, I continue, "Mustard, I think we've been going about this all wrong. We have no hope in finding the lost items. Our chances are better if we look for the elves themselves."

After pausing to laugh at my unintentional rhyme, I dash to the front hall closet to look for my magic tracker. House elves might be good at hiding, but they can't hide from my yellow polka dot umbrella.

"Okay, Mustard, do you want to check upstairs or downstairs first?"

My silly dog doesn't even wait for me to follow, he runs to the top of the stairs, barks, and then continues on running into one of the bedrooms. From the sounds of his paw-steps, I believe he's just jumped on my mother's bed.

"You know you're not supposed to be up there, boy! You better get off Ginger's bed before I get up there!" I call up to him. There's no movement, so I can only assume he didn't hear me.

"Well before I go on my top secret mission to find the thieving house elf, I'll need my night vision goggles. House elves aren't likely to be hiding in the open, now are they?" I roll my eyes as I reach for the sunglasses I keep in my coat pocket, and then I close the folding door before the hall closet contents come exploding out. Wouldn't be the first time, I think to myself.

The night vision goggles come in handy. As soon as I put them on, I feel safer – it's as if I can see more, despite the fact that it's not really night, and it's not really dark. I can immediately see the little dust particles floating about, and I know that my vision is better.

Tapping the side of the glasses, I say, "Thank you, night vision, now find me some mischievous house elves!" I take the steps two at a time, hoping to catch Mustard in the act. He's probably tossing himself about on Mom's comforter, casting her six pillows to the floor, while unmaking her perfectly made bed. As much fun as it is to watch him do this, I know it means I'll have to remake it before Ginger Bean gets home, and there's no time for that.

"Off!" I snap, as soon as I see Mustard. I've busted him tossing the third of the five unnecessary pillows to the floor, but fortunately the comforter is still nicely tucked in at the corners. "We're on an important mission, boy. No time for distractions!"

I pick up all the pillows, fluff them, and delicately return them to their spot. "You check under the bed, Musty; I'll go check the closet. We're looking for a guilty house elf. Do you remember what they look like?"

Mustard begins sniffing under the bed. I'm not entirely sure he remembers our first and only encounter with the magical criminals; for a golden labradoodle, it was quite a long time ago, after all.

Eleven Months Earlier...

I heard a sound coming from the pantry in the kitchen. Naturally I assumed it was mice, because we'd had this problem before. The sound was a lot like creepy old fingernails on a chalkboard... except not on a chalkboard, on a baseboard. Not that it put me on edge, but I still didn't feel right. Mustard was sniffing around the kitchen and into the living room, looking for the culprit, but I was certain the pantry was where the thing would be found.

Without waiting for my faithful sidekick to return, I took the two paces to the pantry and snapped the door open without thinking. It took all my courage not to scream at the image in front of me.

Two large, beady eyes and one long hooked nose within an inch of mine.

"You startled me," the culprit said, and I noticed its fangs right away. The creature hopped off the shelf it'd been standing on, and out of the pantry. Extending its hand, the thing added, "Montgomery Middleton, pleased to meet you."

Despite his sharp fangs, I could see that he meant no harm. Montgomery was polite in offering his hand, so I leaned over just a touch so that I could shake it.

"Britney Fairweather, pleasure is all mine."

Montgomery stood only two feet tall at most, and was much more intimidating when standing on the pantry shelf at eye level.

"Can I help you find something, Mr. Middleton?" I asked, not wanting him to run away before I got the chance to find out what he was up to.

"Monty, please, call me Monty. And yes, I seemed to have lost my way."

"Well, where were you trying to go?"

"My friend, Vanilla LaVille, she told me she lives here but I can't seem to find the entrance way."

"Miss LaVille told you she lives in my pantry?" I asked, trying to watch my tone. I was told that house elves, and at that point that's what I suspected Monty was, are quite fickle.

"Not exactly," he replied.

I waited for him to finish his thought but it ended there.

Well that simply wouldn't do. I prompted for further details. "Well, what exactly did she tell you?"

"Can we sit for a moment?" he asked. "It's quite a long story.

"Where are my manners? Can I make you some tea? Have a seat at the table there; I'll just be a minute."

Monty nodded, smiled, and made his way to the kitchen table. As soon as the water boiled, I put all the fixings together, and served him a make-it-yourself platter. He filled his cup only a quarter full with hot water, and soaked a teabag for exactly two minutes, before removing it with a spoon and eating it.

I resisted the urge to gag. I couldn't believe he just ate the teabag! Out of habit, I tried to follow suit, so as to not offend the mythical being, but I just didn't think my stomach could handle it. Instead, I placed my discarded teabag on my saucer, and added a dollop of milk to my tea.

Monty, seeing me stirring my drink, realized that he could do the same. He reached past the little cup of milk though, and grabbed the bottle of honey instead. Filling his cup to the rim, I wondered how he would stir it, let alone drink it.

One part tea, three parts honey? Gross. Just when I thought it couldn't get any worse, he jumped off the chair, scaled the drawers to the top of the counter, and helped himself to the peppershaker.

Sure that he'd made a mistake, I asked, "You know that's pepper, don't you, Monty?"

"Don't worry, I only use a pinch. It gives my tea a good kick and balances the sweetness of honey."

"Well… okay then."

He hopped off the counter, made his way back to the table, and sure enough, added just a pinch of pepper to his tea. He slid the shaker over to me, as if advising me to do the same. I politely shook my head; I don't like pepper at the best of times.

After stirring his disgusting concoction of what he called tea, he swallowed it down in one large gulp, belched, and excused himself. That time I couldn't suppress my giggle.

"Before I begin my tale," he began, "can you promise we won't be interrupted? I hate being interrupted."

"It really depends on how long the tale is. My mother is at work right now, so she won't be home for at least a couple of hours… and Mustard is upstairs. I can hear him tossing pillows off my mom's bed, so I think he'll be up there a good long while. I'll try to stop him from interrupting, but please, go ahead with your story."

"Have you heard of the Wobble Barn?" he asked me.

"Sorry, Monty, can't say that I have." I sipped my tea as quietly as possible.

"It's a hangout of sorts, I can't say where, as this is top secret. Only the elves can access it, and only if they know the password, which changes regularly."

I nodded as if I understood, and really, I thought I did. It was like a fort, would be my guess.

Monty continued, "So there I was, sitting alone at my regular table in the Wobble Barn, when in walked Vanilla LaVille – only I didn't know her name yet. At just over two feet tall, she was quite unique. I'd never seen a female that tall before. Come to think of it, there's only one elf who reaches that height that I know of. I couldn't stop myself from staring. She was beautiful. Her small ears pointed directly upward like a Doberman, her black eyes were like saucers, and her hair... my goodness, her hair... how she kept it from tangling with the hair on her back was beyond me, but trust me when I say, there is no finer vision than Vanilla LaVille."

It was hard for me not to shudder at the image of back hair, but before I could comment, Monty spoke again.

"Naturally, she didn't even look at me as she crossed the room. I was literally the only elf in the barn apart from the drink-maker, but she pretended not to see me. She headed right to the drink-maker behind the counter and asked for two fingers of rain water."

Monty sighed as if recollecting a dream. If he hadn't warned me about his distaste for interruptions, I would have asked what he meant by 'two fingers of rain water,' but there simply wasn't time.

"The drink-maker, all but drooling, poured her more like four fingers than two, but didn't charge her the difference. In fact, he didn't charge her at all. She winked at him, and he went back to his duties, leaving her to enjoy the four measures of freshly-squeezed Drop."

Ah… a finger is a measurement. Without interrupting, I managed to figure something out. Sometimes, I surprise even myself with my level of brilliance.

"Well, I couldn't just let her sit there alone," Monty said. "I had to join her. I had to find out who she was and what clan she was a part of… you know, the standard stuff we elves talk about upon introduction."

I nodded again, having really no idea about this standard. Taking a break from his storytelling, Monty grabbed the bottle of honey, squeezed a line out onto his long, thin finger, and licked it off delicately.

Since I'm not technically interrupting, because he'd already stopped speaking, I prompted for more. "Well, then what happened?"

"She finished her drink before she spoke to me. She drank slowly too, savouring every last drop – all while pretending I wasn't there. I thought she'd get up and leave without ever acknowledging my presence, but finally, she turned. 'Vanilla LaVille,' she said, her tongue swirling around the letters. You'd think her name was full of R's, the way she rolled it out of her mouth… gosh, I could listen to her say just that and die a happy elf."

Monty lost himself in the memory. He repeated "Vanilla LaVille" so many times; even I had to roll my eyes. I took a sip of my tea and deliberately coughed. Passing it off as a 'went-down-the-wrong-way cough' and not an interruption cough is one of my best tactics.

Fortunately it worked, and the elf continued on with his less than impressive story.

"She asked for my name and clan, but did not give me time to answer. My tongue felt as heavy as bricks, as if my mouth was clamped shut. I was glad she went on and didn't care about my responses; I wasn't in any position to give them. She told the tale about her partner standing her up... about how she lost her shoe in the woods, and I hadn't even noticed she was missing one... about having her wallet disappear, though she was certain it was in the lost shoe... about the troll who she had to pass in order to make it to the Wobble Barn... about the trade she had to make in order to procure her safety... about losing her watch but surviving the encounter... and about the positive outlook that she kept throughout the journey. She ended her tale with 'at least I still have my left shoe, right?'

"This befuddled me." Monty scratched his head like he was still befuddled. "Left shoe right? Right shoe left? Two left shoes? On the right foot? These are the questions that crossed my mind as Vanilla LaVille continued to enchant me with her yarn-weaving and non-existent R-rolling. Whatever it was that she talked about after asking that one simple question was beyond me. I didn't even care; I just wanted her to say her name again and to continue speaking to me. It was the one time I was grateful to be the only elf in the room."

There's a good break in his monologue, and it seems as though he's taking more than a breath between sentences. For this reason, I feel it's safe to ask, "You don't like being alone?"

"Oh no, we elves prefer to travel in pairs. It is perfect when we find our soul mate, but until then, we usually travel with our best mate."

"I assume you don't have a soul mate, else you wouldn't be flirting with Miss Vanilla LaVille. But you don't have a best mate, Monty?"

"Oh, I have a best mate alright. Peter North who hails from the South – he's the funniest elf you'd ever get the opportunity to meet, but most pray they never cross his path."

"Is he dangerous, this Peter North?"

"He can be. If he feels threatened or cornered, he bears his fangs and has been known to use them. He's the meanest elf on the south side of the mountain, but offer him a spot of tea and he'll give you a right ol' laugh in return."

I filed this information away in my memory for future use. Don't corner elves. They have sharp teeth, and they do bite. Peter North is from the South, he's funny but mean and possibly easily threatened, but can be soothed with tea.

I shifted my half-empty cup to the side, no longer wishing to drink. It had gone cold anyway, and I really just wanted to hear Monty's story. "Well, where was Peter North when you met Vanilla LaVille?"

"He was banned from the Wobble Barn for bad behaviour. He was told he needed rehabilitation before he could return. But Peter North is an Elf of the Mountain – he's wild and can never be tamed. We had plans to meet later, but I was positive he wouldn't mind if I spent those hours with Vanilla LaVille instead. That was the only thing I had on my mind at that single moment, and the way the female in front of me kept eyeing me, I knew it was on her mind too."

I knew the elves were frisky by nature, I had no idea how similarly hormonal they were to the teenagers at my high school. Monty might have looked like a two-foot-tall pointy-eared version of E.T., but with all the lights off during movie-time, he could easily pass as one of the boys in my tenth grade class – assuming he could be heard and not seen... Resisting the urge to roll my eyes again, I listened as Monty continued.

"Finally, I found my voice and asked Vanilla to come back to my cove. She was finished her second helping of free rain water; she'd be pushing her luck to ask for a third. Beauty only gets you so far, eventually the drink-maker would ask her to pay and without a wallet, surely she'd ask me – or worse, expect it of me – so I needed to get us both out of the Wobble Barn before that happened.

"It was as if a light bulb went off inside her brain. If I was a Seer by trade, I was sure that I'd have been able to see the flicker of light that appeared above her head. She said, 'Oh, Monty, that's a fabulous idea. But I've just remembered now where I lost my shoe. I must go get it before I forget, or before the tree thieves make off with it. How about you meet me at my cove instead? Does that work for you, Montgomery Middleton?' 'Most certainly it does,' I said in response. You never turn down a lady elf; it is quite an honour to be asked back to one's abode. When courting, it is the male who takes that first step. For a female to do it, well, that meant it was my lucky day!"

"Well?" I couldn't stop myself from interrupting, but his story just got good. He was elated, and that was clearly rubbing off on me as well.

"Well, I'll tell you well – she was two steps to the exit of the Wobble Barn and the silly muckle forgot to give me the address to her cove. She was in such a hurry to get back to the lost shoe that I suppose it hadn't occurred to her that I'd never been to her cove before. She calls out over her shoulder, '1474 Shadowbury Lane, the entrance is through the wooden box in the kitchen,' then she left, tossing her hair aside as she made her way through the door. I finished my drink, gave her ten minutes to find her shoe, and then I followed her to the address she had given to me."

"1474 Shadowbury Lane? That's my house! That's this house! We don't have a wooden box in the kitchen." I paused for just a moment, and then it became clear. "The pantry... you think the entrance to her house is through my pantry – the wooden box in the kitchen – which is why I found you in there."

"Yes, Ma'am Britney, that is correct. I am sure that the entrance to Miss LaVille's is through there. If you just let me be on my way, I won't bother you again."

"I'm sorry, Monty, but I cannot do that. I don't believe you have the right address. There is no cove in my pantry, I promise you."

"But that is the address she gave to me."

"Are you sure? I mean, maybe you heard it wrong? Maybe she said a different number? Though I'm pretty sure that there are no kitchen boxes on the street that lead the way to an elf's home. We probably would have heard about this by now... or there would have been neighbours that sold their homes for fear of what's within... and we've all lived here for over a decade. So no, there are definitely no elves on Shadowbury... are you sure, Monty; are you absolutely sure?"

"Do not mock me, child, what do you know? I heard the address, and as you know, an elf has a good memory – we do. And that was the address that Vanilla LaVille gave me. I promise you that, my friend. We elves get it right – and nobody would forget the address of Ms. Vanilla LaVille!"

"Okay, is it possible she said "Shadow-Berry" maybe that's a different place?"

The elf scratched his chin for a moment. "I suppose, but I don't believe there are any Shadow-Berry Lanes on this side of the mountain, I'd have found them by now. I know this territory like the back of my hand."

It was obvious to me that Monty was telling the truth. It also was obvious that Vanilla LaVille had given him a false address. She seemed like that sort. I mean really, the elf was missing a shoe, a wallet, and a watch, got two drinks for free, and was about to leave the Wobble Barn without giving Monty her address. Clearly she was making a run for it. I just didn't know how to say that respectfully.

"Do you think maybe she didn't want you to know where she lived?"

"Why on earth would she not want me to know that? She invited me there, I didn't ask to go."

"Is it possible then that maybe she didn't know her own address? After all, you have described her as careless. Beautiful, but careless."

Monty scratched his chin again, this time a smile played on his lips. It didn't take a genius to figure out the mischief behind the smile either, but before I could even ask him what was going on, my dog began barking furiously upstairs.

"Mustard!" I didn't hesitate. My trusted companion was very clearly angry – and that's not a common behaviour for him. After grabbing a handful of teabags from the table, stuffing them in my pocket, and clasping Montgomery 'the Liar' Middleton by the wrist so he couldn't escape, I dragged him up the stairs, two at a time, in order to save my dog.

Monty protested, and tried to slow me down, but as it could mean life or death for my favourite thing in the whole wide world, I refused to be thwarted. "You will settle and obey if you know what's good for you, Middleton. It'll hurt less for you in the end, if you comply."

My threat was taken seriously, and Monty picked up speed. He was either worried about what I would do to him should I discover what was wrong with Mustard, or he was tired of hitting his head on the steps and along the floor as I dragged him into my mother's room.

Mustard began growling as I threw open the door. It occurred to me that the door shouldn't have been shut in the first place, since Mustard doesn't open or close doors when he enters or leaves the room, but the reason all became clear when I saw what Mustard was growling at.

There, near the closet was another two-foot-tall elf, this one with yellow eyes, sharp extended fangs, and a hiss that made him sound like a snake.

"Peter North, I presume?"

He hissed his response, yet did not take his eyes off the dog on the bed.

"Let me make this clear, Peter, if you take one step closer to that furry beast, he'll attack... and so will I. You may not care about your life, but what about the life of your best mate?" My grip tightened on Monty, and he yelped.

Threatening isn't something I normally do. I also didn't imagine I'd be any good at it, but nobody threatens my dog. Nobody. We were all at an impasse. Mustard and I may have had the advantage, but a bloodbath on my mother's pristine white sheets would not end well for me, even if I survived the war. I'd certainly incur another when Mom came home from work.

Jaclyn Aurore

I tried a different tactic. "If we all calm down, I'd be happy to offer you some tea." Without letting go of Monty, I reached deep into my pocket and pulled out one solitary teabag, grateful that I had grabbed them before coming to the rescue. I tossed it at Peter's feet and tried again. "Peter, my dog is no fool. He knows you don't belong here, and he's telling you that you need to go. If you go gently, I promise he won't attack. We can have tea, you can explain to me what you are doing in Ginger Bean's closet, and then the two of you can leave – cordially – or such is my preference."

In a heartbeat, Peter's fangs retreated, and he clapped his hands. "Ooh, tea!" He picked up the teabag from the floor and popped it into his mouth. Barely swallowed, he said, "I hope there's more where that came from." He clapped his hands again.

The clapping settled my dog. Well, it was either that, or the lack of fangs and the pleasant smile that replaced the horrid teeth.

"Will you have tea with us, Furry Thing?" Peter said to Mustard.

Mustard replied with a single bark, and we all made our way to the kitchen.

I boiled a new pot of water and offered the same platter to Peter that I had to Monty earlier. Both elves followed the routine that Monty had: soak bag in a quarter cup of hot water, eat bag, pour three quarters of a cup of honey into the quarter cup of tea, add a pinch of pepper, chug the contents of the cup, belch, and smile.

The dog gave me a funny look, and I couldn't say I blamed him. Instead of joining in, or even pouring myself, or Mustard, a cup of regular tea, I watched the two elves, lest they tried any more tricks.

"Peter North, now that you've had your tea, I'd like to know what you were doing in my mother's closet... please," I added as an afterthought. These elves were up to no good, and I didn't much care for them. Manners are not something easily remembered at times like that.

"I thought I'd offer a gift to the Lady LaVille," he said, reaching for another teabag. "The invitation to her home was not extended to me. For me to just show up unannounced, the least I could do is off her something of value."

"So it's true then." At this point, I turned my attention to my faithful dog, who was sitting on guard next to my feet. "I thought they were just thieving our things. Monty was caught red-handed in the pantry, and you caught Peter in the closet. I had truly believed the story of Vanilla LaVille was a fabrication. A story that Monty came up with on the spot to distract me while Peter made off with the more valuable goods."

Peter immediately began to growl, and I knew that I'd offended him. But his growling offended my dog, and so Mustard began growling too. Reminding the elves that I did catch them both in the act of thieving, I didn't think I owed anyone an apology. Monty distracted his friend by shoving a homemade biscuit into his mouth.

"Ooh, this is absolutely divine!" Peter said, crumbs flying out of his mouth.

"Thanks, I helped my mother make those."

When he'd finished licking his lips, Peter explained, "We elves are an honest bunch. We don't lie, cheat, or steal. We are not criminals. I've heard you call us this before, Britney Fairweather, but you are wrong."

I was slightly concerned that Peter knew my name, since I knew that I never gave it to him. It made me wonder how many times he'd been to my house and just how much snooping he'd done.

"My apologies, Peter… but what did you expect to find in Ginger Bean's closet to give to Vanilla LaVille, that you wouldn't have had to steal?"

"Memories. Let me explain how it works because you, fair Fairweather, know not as much as you think. Everything in the human world has a memory attached. Articles of clothing generally have the most memories within them, because they see much more. As spinners of yarn, we elves enjoy these memories; they help us to embellish or give good material to our next tale."

I nodded my head, and so did Mustard. This was all very interesting.

Monty picked up where Peter stopped. "A memory can be taken from an inanimate object by one of three ways. We can wear the item, but this only works if the item is clothing—"

Peter interrupted Monty with a cackle of a laugh. "Oh, Monty, can you imagine if we walked around wearing those big wooden tables as hats?" He flipped over the platter in front of him, so that everything that was on it ended up on the table, and he balanced the empty platter on his head, while crossing his eyes and sticking out his long, slender tongue.

Monty laughed so hard he fell off of his chair. When he regained composure he said to me, "What did I tell you about this guy? I said he was funny, didn't I?" He slapped his knee and continued to laugh.

"Hysterical," I said, shaking my head and rolling my eyes at Mustard. The dog mimicked my behaviour to a tee, telling me that he, too, thought Monty may have exaggerated about Peter's comic ability – or their sense of humour was nothing like ours.

After Peter took the tray off of his head, he reached for another biscuit, and plopped it into his mouth. Without the distraction, Monty was able to continue. "Another way that we retrieve memories is by breathing them in. This takes a little bit longer, and much more control."

When Peter was finished his treat, he demonstrated this as well. Closing his eyes, he put his forehead to the platter on the table and began to breathe heavily. We all watched quietly until the process was done. It was bizarre; even I knew when the elf had retrieved the memories from the platter. The shine had been sucked out – or maybe that was just my imagination – but I was certain I saw a glow around the platter while Peter was deep breathing, and then the glow was gone.

With the smile on his face, Peter said, "This silver tray has more to it than meets the eye. It has served tea for generations. Your great, great grandmother used this platter to serve tea to the man courting her. Once married, she only served tea using this very same platter. Her husband became accustomed to seeing his tea this way, and once said to her that he'd never have tea any other way. She laughed, but he kept to his word and admitted that other than at home with his wife, he never accepted a spot of tea from anyone." Peter's eyes snapped back to present time. "Such a shame. That declaration cost him many a good drink, but he did seem happy with his decision, so more power to him."

"You got all that from sniffing the tray?" I asked. "Fascinating. What's the third way to take memories from things?"

"Elves only practice those two ways. It requires dark magic for the third method," Monty answered.

Peter scoffed while saying, "and a magic wand."

"Memories are tricky things," Monty continued, ignoring

Peter altogether. "If not done correctly, or if done too often, breathing in another's memory can replace your own. It's why we have to be at least one hundred and fifty years of age before we're even taught how to do it. The younger elves just stick to items that can be worn. These stolen memories are not ours to keep. Once we use them, they are discarded, or transferred to the next elf."

"What does that mean?" I covered my mouth with both hands, realizing my mistake. I shouldn't have interrupted Monty; it could have put him in a foul mood.

Thankfully, he didn't notice. It was almost as if having the comfort of his best mate put him at ease.

"It means that once transferred, the memory is of no use to the original elf, but the elf or elves who hear the memory treat it as one of their own, with no harm done. We are never at risk of losing our own memories when we hear them from someone else, only when they are stolen directly."

"So the memory that Peter took from the silver platter has been transferred to you now?" I ask.

"Yes, I am free to tell that tale, though not very interesting, to as many people as I wish. It is stuck with me now, but Peter has already forgotten. He used it up."

I looked to Peter for confirmation. He shrugged and nodded.

"So you don't recall the story of my great, great grandmother?"

"The memory is gone, child," Peter responded.

Turning my attention back to Monty, I said, "Well if you still remember, can you not just repeat the tale back to him?"

"You think you're so clever, Britney Fairweather. Do you not think we tried this already? Of course we cannot! I mean, I can repeat the tale all I want, but Peter won't be able to register it. It's like his mind will take in all the words I say and then garble them up, replacing them with a tale he's already heard."

Peter added, "This is why it is so dangerous for the young. If they go about breathing in memories, and doing so incorrectly, those memories will replace their own. Once they share what they have learned, it is gone from their mind, but their memories do not come back."

It was Monty's turn to nod as he said, "They are emptying their minds, the poor wee buggers. They get downright stupid... much like the trolls, only smaller."

"If they're really unlucky, they can lose their way home and wander straight into the trolls' den." As Peter spoke, this time it seemed he was recalling his own memory. "The troll would show kindness to the elf child, thinking it is his own. But when the elf fails to grow beyond his two-feet, the troll will show kindness no more and eat the elf for dinner."

"That's horrible!" I gasped, once again covering my mouth, this time from shock.

"Such is part of our life. This happens more so than we care to admit." Monty shook his head and looked at his lap.

I wondered briefly if he'd lost someone dear to him.

It was Peter that snapped me out of it. "Do not feel remorse, child. We teach the young the dangers of memory-breathing. They don't learn how to do this by being taught. It's the children who spy who think they know what they've seen. They attempt to do it, and since they've acquired a memory, they assume they've done it correctly. They have no knowledge of the memory they lost in the process. We tell them to stick with clothing – to just wear the item and return it, but the stubborn children are just that. Stubborn."

Something else became clear at that moment. "Okay, so you say that you are not thieves. You only take memories, and since you are taking them from inanimate objects, there's really no harm done. It's not as if you are taking memories directly from the human—"

"Absolutely not!" Monty interrupted. "That's not possible. Even if we wanted to, we wouldn't be able to. But there is a strict rule against it. It's part of our honour code. We don't lie, we don't cheat, we don't steal, and we don't get within three feet of the humans."

"But you are here, speaking with me."

"You are not entirely human." Seeing the look on my face, Peter added, "If you were, you wouldn't be able to see us, for one. And also, I know who your father is. I found that memory while I was in that ginger woman's closet."

"My father was an honourable man. He died when I was young but not so young that I don't remember him."

"No, silly girl, that man was your stepfather. I found that memory too, but it's not as interesting."

"Well, good then. If it's not interesting, then you won't mind losing it. Share the memory with me, Peter. Please… I need to know."

He sighed and turned to his friend. "Do we have time? When is Vanilla LaVille expecting you?"

"No time was established. I'm quite certain she has forgotten. If it'll ease the child, you should tell her what she needs to know – else she'll sick the furry beast on us."

Peter looked to Mustard, who licked his lips as if to agree with what Monty had just said, and then turned to me. "Very well, but you may not like what I have to say, and you cannot unhear it."

"I can handle it, I promise."

"Your father, or the man you knew to be your father, was still courting your mother when you were conceived. He believed you to be his, and so he married your mother and the two lived quite happily. Your mother, however, knew otherwise."

"She cheated on my dad? No way!"

"According to the memory," Peter continued like I hadn't spoken, "your mother was visited in the middle of the night by a strange... presence."

"What kind of presence?" I ask. Did he mean an elf? Was my real father an elf? That might explain why I'm so short despite my mother being the beanpole that she is.

"This is unclear. She only remembers it as a presence. But the only presences known to lurk in the night and stir the humans while they sleep are the Dallywags, or more commonly known as male pixies."

"A pixie? You are confused, Peter, even I know that pixies are small and can sit in the palm of my hand should I be lucky enough to catch one."

"This is true, but they have the ability to present themselves as human whenever the need should arrive," Peter stated this like it should be obvious to me.

For good measure, Monty added, "And sometimes they do so when there is no need."

Placing both my hands on the table to stop from falling off my chair, I repeated what I've heard so far, "So you're saying my real dad is a pixie or a dillywog."

"Dallywag! And at this point, it's just an assumption." It was Peter who clarified. "Your mother's memory showed that before you, she was unable to conceive. The presence in the room did something magic, and soon after she was told that she was pregnant. She assumed the presence was Heavenly, and became quite religious for a while."

"She's still religious. That never changed."

"Maybe so, but in the memory, she started to doubt that the presence was Heavenly. After some time, she became unsure. Her faith in the Higher Being, the one you call 'God', grew strong, but she never felt worthy to be a chosen one and so…"

"So, she assumed that the presence was a myth of some kind," I finished, "which is why she gives me such a hard time when I start telling my stories. She doesn't ever want me to accidentally hit the nail on the head… though I have to say, I never in a million years would have suspected that I was half-pixie… or half-Dallywag, or whatever. This is by far the craziest thing I've ever heard!"

"And with that, we need to bid you adieu. Vanilla LaVille will eventually realize that she extended an invite to me, and I do not wish to stand that lady elf up. She is one of a kind." Monty hopped of the chair and made his way to the pantry.

Peter made to follow but turned his attention to me once more. "Do remember, child, no matter what presence your mother felt, Higher Being, Dallywag, or Crimson Unicorn, you are a half-breed of something magical. If not, you wouldn't be able to see us."

The two elves made their way to the middle shelf of my kitchen pantry, and before I had the wits about me to tell them they still had the wrong address, they clapped their hands and disappeared in a puff of smoke… but not smoke… cookie dust.

If they hadn't disappeared the way they did, I would have told them that I thought Ms. Vanilla LaVille was a young elf who hadn't listened to what she was taught, tried to breathe in memories, and lost her own. That was the only way I could justify how clueless she appeared to be... and yet... and yet she seemed to get her address right because the elves did indeed pass through some portal in the wooden box in my kitchen.

The more cookie dust I inhaled, the more clueless I felt. Was I accidentally breathing in memories before I was taught the proper way to do so? Did I need to wait another hundred years before I could breathe in memories properly? Was I even able to take memories from inanimate objects? Can Dallywags do that? Or just elves? The more questions I asked myself, the worse I felt. It felt like nausea was consuming me, and the last thing I remember was Mustard barking.

Present Day...

The dog is pretty good at alerting me to danger, so when he starts barking I snap my attention away from the memory of Peter North and Montgomery Middleton, and into the present day.

"What is it, boy? Did you find them?" I naturally assume it's the same two elves, although it really shouldn't be. After they left, I pasted a note in the back of the cupboard that banned all house elves from travelling into my house, pantry or not, I didn't want to see one ever again.

And yet here I am, searching for house elves using my night vision goggles, and listening to the cues of my dog. He's found something in my mother's closet that has him on edge.

"If that's you, Monty, you better go. Same with you, Peter. I won't stop my dog from eating either of you this time… and I'm not offering tea!"

Mustard starts scratching his paws on the carpet frantically. I need to know what he's looking for. The only time I've ever seen him do this is when he's outside in the backyard burying his dog toys and treats. I get down on all fours and join him at the base, pretending to dig up dirt because that's what he's doing. I want to help him because I feel that he's trying to help me.

Sure enough, I find the source of his anxiety. There is a piece of carpet that is loose from the rest. It peels up like a flap, and underneath is a wooden floorboard. "Well, that was a lot of hype over nothing, Mustard. It's just more flooring, relax."

But the dog continues to bark and nudge at my hand, and I realize why. The flooring is loose as well… like there's a plank of wood that just doesn't belong. Breaking a nail trying to lift the piece, I cry out in pain but am determined as ever to get to the bottom of this… literally.

When the piece of wood finally pops out, I am only half surprised at what I find… a jar of nutmeg, a bunch of cookies that came from the cookie jar, and a stash of teabags.

"House elves. Bloody house elves. Sure, they don't steal, but they do move stuff around the house making it difficult for you to find it later. It's some stupid game they play. Well, go on then, Mustard. Eat the cookies. I'm not hungry anymore."

Pulling out all the cookies and leaving them for Mustard to consume, I also remove all the other things that shouldn't be there, put the board back, followed by the carpet, and just as I'm leaving the room, I hear, "Britney!"

"Yes, Mom? I'm up here!"

"Okay, sweetie, I just wanted you to know I'm home now."

"That's great... And you should know that I found the nutmeg," I say to her as I walk down the stairs.

"Where was it?" she asks, as I hand her the jar, which still has plenty of nutmeg left in it for more baked goods.

"It rolled under the fridge. Mustard sniffed it out."

Jaclyn Aurore

Britney Fairweather and the Flightless Bird

Ginger Bean, also known as 'Mom', recently grounded me for tardiness. For two weeks, I have to come straight home from school, no taking 'shortcuts' through The Enchanted Forest, no taking the dog for extra long walks, no nothing. I guess one too many times my shortcuts turned into adventures that lasted hours instead of minutes. *Oops. Sorry, Ginger Bean.*

While walking home from school the boring way – along sidewalks and main streets – I happen to hear an unfortunate chirping. Not the normal bird song; this sounds more like a wounded cry. My heart sinks. I need to find this animal and try to help – even if it means going home late and risking the wrath of Ginger.

Following the sounds of squeaking and squawking, I finally find the source. A red-breasted bluebird, lying on the curb of the road, is frantically flapping its wings, yet not able to take flight. There doesn't appear to be anything wrong with the bird, except its proximity to a storm drain. It's a mostly sunny day, so this bluebird shouldn't be so panicked about being washed down the drain. However, a nearby house must have had a flood or something. There's a

85

long purple tube coming from around the back of the house, and it's flushing out water like a tsunami.

"Poor little bird," I say, as I slowly reach for the quivering creature. "I'm not allowed in the forest today, but I will take you as close as I can." As I reach for it, the thing flaps and flaps. "No silly bird. I'm here to help."

Once safely in my hands, the bird begins to settle its wings, but does not stop the insufferable squawking.

"Now I understand why Ginger said no to birds. What is it you're so upset about? If you're scared of me, why not just fly away?"

With that, the bluebird buried its beak inside its red feathers. I'm no good at understanding birds unless they speak to me – but if I had to guess, I'd say this one looked ashamed.

Using the pad of one finger, I pat the bird's head and stroke lightly down its back. "It's okay, Bluebird. I will do my best to help."

In response, the bird untucks its beak and rests its head on the palm of my hand, chirping just once, as if it understands. Having lost a little time already, and not wanting to upset the Ginger Bean any further, I begin to quicken my step. We aren't far from the edge of The Enchanted Forest, just one turn off a backstreet, and voilà.

Kneeling, I place the bird on the ground at the base of a tree and ask, "Will you be alright, Mr. Bluebird?" not expecting a response.

To my surprise, the bird nods and chirps. "Thank you, Britney Fairweather, Child Who Sees."

"You can talk?" This surprises me more than the little animal knowing my name. It seems all the creatures of The

Enchanted Forest have heard of me, and often refer to me as "Child Who Sees".

"I've gbeen talking to you this whole time, child. When I realized you didn't understand, I stopped trying."

"But I understand you now. It must be because we've crossed over the magical border." Not wanting to violate probation, I had placed the bluebird inside the forest's edge, while kneeling on the outside. The way, Ginger can't say I disobeyed.

"Yes, this is probably so. I won't dare venture out again."

"Why not, Bluebird? Many of your feathered friends travel in and out of the woods all the time – though I've never seen one with such vibrant colours."

The bird flaps its wings with pride, but still does not rise from the ground.

"Unlike the birds you see, I was born inside the forest, atop a large oak tree. What I didn't realize, until today, is that I am blessed and cursed along with the magic within the realm. I cannot leave it."

After scratching my head in confusion, I look at my watch. I don't have time for a story, but I need to understand this small bird's predicament. "But you did leave… else, how would I have found you moments before you were washed down the drain?"

"I was flying high above the ground when I lost my bearings. As soon as I left the border, I could no longer fly. I plummeted to the earth, but with my wings spread wide, I was able to glide to a safe landing. Fortunately, I didn't break anything in the fall, but I am sore. I will need time to mend before I can fly again. It should be easier for me to heal here in The Enchanted Forest."

"Okay, Mr. Bluebird. Be safe! No more flying outside these trees, then. I do have to go. My mom will be upset if she finds me dilly-dallying and socializing with animals."

"Before you go, Britney Fairweather. I have a gift for you." Again, the bluebird tucks his beak into his breast. His head bobs just slightly, and with a small chirp, he pulls a red feather from his chest. He places the feather in the palm of my hand and says, "Thank you, child, for bringing me home. May this token of appreciation bring you luck when you need it most."

I tap the bird's head lightly, affectionately. "Thank you for the gift," I reply, rising from my kneeling position. "Maybe I'll see you again soon!"

And with that, I run home, hoping Ginger won't be too upset about my tardiness. Just to be on the safe side, I silently wish upon my lucky red feather.

About the Author

Jaclyn Aurore is the author of *The Starsville Saga (Starting Over, Standing Up, Giving In, Hanging On, Leaving Behind)*, and is currently writing the stand alone fantasy, *My Life Without Me*.

Her books have been described as "Wonderfully human", "Evokes the awkwardness of teenage life perfectly", "Heart-wrenching and heartwarming at the same time". She is a wife and mother, and lives in Ontario, Canada.

When she's not redecorating her home for the hundredth time, you can find Jaclyn at Starbucks, frappuccino in hand, working on her next novel.

Connect with Jaclyn:

Website **http://www.jaclynaurore.com/**
Facebook: **https://www.facebook.com/JaclynAurore**
Twitter: **@JaclynAurore**